THE EVER-DARK

THE INDIRETTAN CHRONICLES
BOOK 1

EL HOFFMAN

Content Note

The Ever-Dark is classified as new adult literary fantasy and contains references to mental health, mild fantasy violence, brief sexual suggestiveness, one strong word, and mild drug and alcohol use by secondary characters.

N
W
E
S
Witch Island
Bridge to Nowhere
Greensfeld
Walled City
Lighthouse
Apple Orchard
Crater Lake
Amberlet
cherry bridge
Ruth's Pond
Aria
Oasis
Circa

"LOVE"

Love is like a winding road by a stream
It's the magic in a dream
Hoping it's not filled with sorrow
Waiting each day until tomorrow
Hoping everything is bright
Praying your path is winding right
Filling my eyes with the light
Smiling now and forever again
When?

- El Hoffman

CHAPTER 1

Loved by no one and disliked by nearly everyone, nineteen-year-old Violet Evans stared at her reflection in the mirror. While she found herself pleasant to look at with her shoulder-length, gently wavy hair the color of walnuts, complete with a pale complexion and striking hazel eyes; she felt the weight of her solitude crushing down on her heavily. The sting of betrayal from her closest friend, Lysander, hung heavy in her heart. For years, she had cherished their bond, only to be cast aside unceremoniously as he forsook her and sought the company of another woman. It wasn't love she sought from him, but the simple comfort of companionship, and his abandonment left her adrift in a sea of isolation.

Pressing her hands on the sides of the mirror frame, she thought about her own sisters, who should be her allies in a world that seemed determined to snub her. They had turned their backs, leaving her to wander the woods alone every day, yearning for solace and sanctuary to read her books. Acknowledging that it was May 6th, Lysander's birthday, she sighed, thinking that she couldn't wish him a happy birthday after what he put her through. She walked out of the house, seeking refuge to read her novels within nature's embrace.

Though not unpleasant to look at, the world around Violet mimicked her internal solitude and deeply rooted sadness—dull, drab, and boring, a place she would describe as lifeless, painted in endless shades of beige. It felt isolated, with nothing noteworthy coming in or out. Her surroundings, composed of cold stone and worn wooden structures, offered little comfort—a perfect backdrop to her lonely existence.

Her knowledge of her region and continent was somewhat limited; most people in her village, Circa, had no idea what lay beyond its borders. It was exceptionally rare to see a stranger's face—perhaps only at the pub, though she had never ventured there herself. She did know of a fishing village that she imagined had trade routes. If such routes existed, she wasn't aware of them; they must not have traded with her village, as everything in Circa was local, and not much came in or out. If the trade routes did carry goods, they most certainly didn't carry people—or so she believed.

In any case, the fishing village was a distant place said to be filled with riffraff, best avoided according to her late parents. She had no idea what lay between her village and the west, and she had always been told there was nothing beyond the woods northeast of her home.

The woods were only barely north, and she had heard that things simply stopped just east of them—with no awareness of anything further.

As she noticed her neighbor Andrew, with his crazed demeanor and frequently jittery movements, walking down the path, a sharp pain seared through her temples and forehead, a physical echo of the emotional turmoil she endured. How could the indifference of her own flesh and blood induce such distress in the form of a migraine?

Her neighbor approached and said "Hi Violet!" Mentally rolling her eyes, she chose to entertain him despite the migraine. "I'm doing it, I'm going to Aria today, Miss Violet." Andrew claimed to be going to a place called Aria every time they spoke. He had something wrong with him and was the bane of the town's existence, but he didn't know that. Her one-room schoolhouse, the Bible, and local myths and legends had never taught her of such a place. Even if such a place existed, she didn't believe ship crossings were accessible for those in her village, and other than by foot, they had no other method of travel. From her understanding, those in Circa did not venture far from home.

"Good for you, Andrew! Let me know how Aria is, alright?" Physically rolling her eyes this time, she muttered to herself, "I would love to go to Aria if such a place existed. Anywhere but here would be a great change of pace," then continued walking and entered the forest on the edge of town, where she spent her days reading. The forest, while drab, was quite beautiful in some respects. The umbrella pines, also known as stone pines or pinus pinea, were beloved by those who entered the forest. Moving at a brisk pace now, ready to have some time to herself, she walked toward a location whispered about in old stories from time to time—the Crater Lake. Glistening blue, the waters contrasted with the monotony of her world and, she felt, her life as a whole. She often spent time near the lake in various spots, feeling "peaceable" as she called it as a child. It was the only body of water nearby that she was aware of. From what she had learned, the lake had been there before her ancestors' time, and she wondered if they had witnessed the fall of the fiery star believed to have created the lake. She often wondered if the supposed celestial event changed everything around it, but her life was too dreadful to give that much consideration.

CHAPTER 2

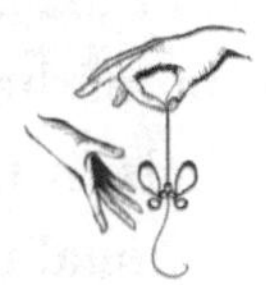

Finding a moss-covered log just beyond the lake that seemed to offer a potential moment of peace, she noticed a peculiar glimmering light beckoning from between two stone pine trees. Intrigued yet skeptical, she stepped between the trees. Instantly, she knew something was wrong, because when she turned around, the shimmering had vanished. It was replaced by darkness like none she had ever seen. Was this still part of Circa, some forgotten corner of it, or had she somehow wandered into a place entirely unfamiliar? She couldn't tell. Somewhat content to be away from her wretched sisters and feeling a sense of a reversal of fate as if things could change for the better, she started walking forward. After walking a few miles, the treeline started to thin. Up ahead, she noticed a bridge over a small greenish-blue lake, with an assortment of strange-looking bicycles lined up in rows along the side of the bridge. Her steps slowed as she stopped to process what she was seeing. These weren't like the bicycles she knew—simple contraptions with two equal-sized wheels, powered by petals and a chain drive and meant for a single driver. The bicycle-like machines in front of her seemed excessively elaborate, with two wheels in the back and what appeared to be seats for additional riders. Some had a curved canopy on the top as if to block the sun while others did not, and some had a fully enclosed cab as if there was a miniature room atop the back of the bicycle. There was a small sign stating "pedicab pickup point," but she wasn't quite sure what that meant.

"Pedicab?" she whispered the word aloud, pondering if that was what she was seeing in front of her. It must have been, as there were so many and of different vari-eties. Where she grew up, bicycles were a newer method of equipment, as the pedals and chains were only recently added, and more of her neighbors were able to acquire them in the recent years. These bicycles seemed to do more than the intended purpose that she knew of, seemingly an indulgence where a servant might cart those of high standing around.

Confused yet fascinated, she cautiously stepped onto the bridge. Further down the bridge, she spotted one of the unusual vehicles that she now believed was called a pedicab. Its driver was lounging in the back, seemingly lost in a cloud of acrid-smelling smoke. The sight of the lone figure stirred a cautious hope within her, as if this encounter might hold the promise of understanding or even kinship in this bewildering realm. Because of this, her curiosity drew her closer, and as she approached, the pedicab driver sat up straighter and his eyes met hers.

"Welcome to the Cherry Bridge, miss," he said, his voice tinged with an air of mystery. "I am Kazuki, your guide to this enchanted realm. Shall we embark on a journey together?"

Although she didn't have anything better to do, she hesitated, unsure of this stranger's intentions. However, something in Kazuki's eyes resonated with her, and she decided to trust her instincts.

"What is this contraption?" she asked, gesturing to the pedicab. "It's unusual. Where I come from, bicycles are new and carry only the person who pedals themselves around." Kazuki laughed and got out of the back of the pedicab, now leaning against the side of it.

"Ah, you are speaking of mortal bicycles! Very simple devices that take a single rider on a single journey. Here, bicycles do exist, but we also have these vehicles of connection. These pedicabs are meant to provide transport to more than one rider, often for an exchange of coins. Your journey today is of no charge, though, miss. Are you ready to set off?" With a nod, she climbed aboard the pedicab, and they set off, traversing the bridge into the unknown.

Away they rode into the mystical realm, and she felt content with a sense of tranquility—although she was still somewhat cautious. On the other side of the lake, more stone pine forest, with a path leading through it, came into view. They continued, and she realized that Kazuki seemed to be able to sense her thoughts and desires. He knew something was bothering her, but she wasn't ready to specify what thoughts were swirling through her mind. They moved forward in silence until they entered a small hamlet with a small wooden sign designating it as Amberlet, population 60. It was nearing nightfall, and the waning night of dusk bathed the landscape. Feeling vulnerable, she realized she couldn't turn back, but she had nowhere to stay and nothing to eat. Kazuki told her that her journey ended there, and she disembarked. As she and Kazuki bid farewell with him stating "Follow the stars, Violet, because they will light the way wherever you go," she felt a deep sense of gratitude for the ride they shared and the companionship, if just for a short time. Wonder and curiosity enveloped her, and she watched as he turned back toward the edge of the forest along the lakeshore, his enigmatic presence igniting a spark of intrigue within her. Left to navigate the unfamiliar hamlet alone, she wandered, awestruck by the inexplicable allure and the mysteries that seemed to have unfolded right before her eyes. The realization that the entirety of this enchanting realm had been concealed within the mundane confines of the forest filled her with an inexplicable sense of wonder and unease.

While exploring, she saw a crow seated high up in a nearby tree. They made eye contact, and then the crow eerily cried out what seemed to be a prophecy:

"Hear ye, heed ye, the foolish deed,
Of heart unwise and reckless need.
The sun begins, but shall not stay,

No noontime high in the month of May,
And all the world in twilight lay."

She spotted what appeared to be an inn just down the way, so she gently opened the door and stepped inside. A short, goblin-like man occupied the receptionist's desk, and asked whether she'd be renting a room by the hour or by the night. Concerned, she made it clear that she was an honest woman and would rent by the night. Flippantly, the goblin-like man explained that his name was Sparrow and that she must not be from around these parts.

"Twenty shekels for the night, ma'am," he said. She was confused, as she hadn't known of a shekel outside of the Bible, and she didn't know the conversion rate from Circa's currency.

Quivering slightly, she asked "What's a shekel?" and he held out his hand, showcasing three bronze or copper-like penny-shaped coins with a left-facing sickle embossed on them.

"Them's a shekel, ma'am, have you got amnesia?" He asked. She explained that she journeyed from out of town, but would gladly pay with the currency she had or perhaps make a trade of some kind. He rolled his eyes, as if something on the ceiling absolutely fascinated him, and told her that unless she finds an un-gentleman or two to rent a room with her by the hour or perhaps by the night, she'd best find lodging elsewhere. Modest and intending to stay that way, she made haste, walking briskly down the quiet, empty, and dark street. Moving on, she reached the outskirts of town and walked until she noticed a somewhat dilapidated barn off the main road. She thought that would be better lodging than a whorehouse or a storefront bench and approached it quietly. Peeking through the crack in the door, she didn't notice anyone inside. It appeared abandoned. Apart from some long-forgotten hay on the ground in one stall, the barn was empty and filled with dust and stale, stagnant air. Better than nothing, she supposed, and prepared to sleep on a bed of hay for the night. Sleeping fitfully from the hard ground and pokey straw, the night passed without incident other than the discomfort. When morning came, she realized she needed to either continue on or return to a household with sisters who treated her like a servant and figuratively spat on her. She chose the former, and intended to move quickly before the midday sun appeared and showcased her trespassing in the dilapidated barn. Before she could think further, a burly and shirtless man swung open the barn door, carrying a bottle of wine and a baguette. She ducked back in the corner of her stall, covering herself with straw and hoping to remain unseen. For hours she waited, while she watched the not unattractive man drink his alcohol and eat his fill of bread. She had never liked alcoholic men and tried to stay away from most males, wanting to protect her virtuous nature while she could. She couldn't help but gaze out between the straw though, and she thought about what it would be like for him to ask the innkeeper if he could rent a room for a few hours with her.

No, she thought, "I shouldn't think such disgraceful

thoughts at this time. I need to find safe lodging, an escape from my past, and perhaps a trade in knitting or child-watching. I have no time for thoughts of marriage or what happens between bedsheets, she thought. I need to find a way out of this barn, unseen."

What must have been hours later, as the dark-haired farmer seemed to have dozed, he awoke and left the barn, leaving the empty bottle to be forgotten. Unsure why he entered the barn in the first place, she collected her thoughts and what was left of her sanity, opened the barn door just barely, glanced left and right, and ran like a madwoman until the barn was out of sight.

"Should I go back home?" Violet thought to herself. What would be the point when she wasn't wanted or welcomed by her sisters? She didn't know where she was, and was surrounded by people she didn't know and a world she wasn't familiar with, but she had to carry on despite it all.

As she walked through the thinning tree line, she caught sight of two men on the edge of her vision. Friends, perhaps, or potentially a couple? They glanced her way with unreadable expressions filled with something she couldn't quite place—suspicion, or maybe just curiosity. They were only strangers, yet they seemed to regard her in a way that unsettled her. She quickly looked away, focusing on the path ahead, but the encounter caused her thoughts to drift to her family.

She had two siblings and two parents. She was told that her parents, Patricia and Bal, both passed away from an illness that swept through Circa a decade ago. Her elder sisters Isabella and Margaret, in that order, had never taken a liking to her. As a child, she was told that she shouldn't exist because she made them share and that they'd rather she not be there at all. After their parents died, it was just the three of them. Isabella and Margaret had it out for her, always stating that her existence killed their family. Violet frequently spent her evenings poring over maps, determined to escape. She flitted around, finding quiet spots to read in peace. Oftentimes that took place near the Crater Lake, but not today.

She thought that she wished to forget. Maybe she could belong in this place of strange coins and odd creatures if she didn't remember where she came from—or the pain of not being loved by those who should love her most. But would it be best to have never experienced her pain and have been born somewhere other than Circa, to forget the pain and be presumed to be from this strange place, or to remember what happened despite the frequent pain? It was a thought she often pondered when alone, before resorting to reading as a distraction.

Determined to find comfortable accommodations, she decided that the next town might have better options for her. She set off, hoping that northwest would take her to better places. Following a stream off the trail for some time, she saw what appeared to be Kazuki and his pedicab, stopped to rest off the side of the path. "Is this a sign? Am I meant to continue on in this direction?" she thought.

Why, it *was* Kazuki. She crept closer until he noticed

her, stating that he was waiting for her. "Why did you take so long?" he asked.

Unsure what he meant or why he thought that, she asked why he felt that way. He stated, "I can feel you from far away, for our conversation drew out your inner self. I'm aware of many people, although I don't say that often. You have a kind face, so you can know the truth."

She was very concerned, at a pivotal state of life but without experience in life's challenges other than an overall state of melancholy. Her self-reliance thus far was built out of necessity rather than choice, and now she was entirely alone and in an unfamiliar and other-worldly place. Outside of the innkeeper she'd rather avoid and the barnman she wasn't acquainted with, it was just Kazuki she knew here. If she was meant to trust anyone, she felt it must be this strange psychic traveler with his smoke-filled cab. If she was meant to journey on, it must be with him, she thought. "Okay, but where are we meant to go?" she asked.

Kazuki chuckled, "Away from here. Don't worry, my kingdom is contrary to this and much different from your neck of the woods as well."

She didn't know how he knew where she was from, but she naively saw no reason to doubt. He stabilized his cab and gently guided it back on the main path before beckoning her inside. "How long is this journey?" She asked, "and why was I left in the hamlet?"

Again he chuckled, "You'll see, and I abandoned you because there was someone you had yet to meet." What was that supposed to mean? That was not an answer, or not one she would fancy to accept.

"Who might that be? The goblin innkeeper who tried to threaten my morals, or the shirtless man who drank wine in the barn?" Kazuki didn't answer, continuing to pedal on. After a long period of silence, she saw the hazy outline of a castle with many turrets, a high wall, and many small and moderate houses. Much larger than Amberlet or Circa, this must be a city like she had read about. "Where are we, strange psychic?" Kazuki continued in silence, leaving her perplexed.

As they rode to the gates underneath a sign stating Greensfeld, Kazuki's cab came to a stop. He disembarked, and held out his hand to help her do the same. Before letting go of her fair hand, he took his other hand and placed a bag heavy with coins on top of her palm. "What's this?" she asked.

He told her not to rent rooms by the hour, that she would find much better than that in this sickle-coined world. "Your dues for humoring me, and enduring my long-winded silence. Farewell for now, Miss Princess. You'll understand soon why the trees had a sparkling aura. Don't be concerned."

She was mystified, unsure of where to begin speaking or what to say. Before she could form a word, Kazuki got back on his pedicab, winked, and threw his cloak and short-brimmed hat towards her before peddling off. She pondered why she would need new wares, but she was grateful that the cloak contained an inner pocket for her change, and the cap was comfortable if slightly big.

She walked the last few feet towards the gates, and swung one open, looking back at the dust where her driver once was. Not thinking about him for a moment longer, she shut the gate and stared in awe at the sight ahead of her. The city of her dreams, right in front of her! Oh how wondrous.

Fortunately, an inn was just up ahead and to the left. "Oh, I hope it's not like the last one I came across," she thought to herself. Striding up to the door, she said a quick thought in her head and opened the door. Another goblin-like man spoke, asking how many nights she would like to rest her head.

"At least four, enough to right myself and get my bearings," she said. That should be enough for now, she thought to herself.

"That shall be 100 shekels, madam. Does the third floor fancy you?"

She counted out the right amount and stated that any floor is better than no floor. In exchange for the coins, he handed her a weighty gold-toned key. "304, dear," she was told, and she turned and ventured up the stairs. Although she had nothing except the clothes on her back and her newfound coins, hat, and cloak, she set those on the bed.

"My, what a strange two days have gone by." She decided to turn in for the evening, and would decide on another course of action the following day.

After a restful night's sleep, she awoke to a rooster crowing from what sounded like just outside. She stretched and rose, putting her cloak on once more. She remembered that she needed new wares other than those Kazuki had given to her. She thought that would be a good first stop. A seamstress must be close by in a city such as this, she thought. After walking up and down a few streets and alleys, she saw a window with a sign picturing a needle and thread. She entered the store, and was greeted by a woman with a striking, pale-skinned face, bent hook nose, vivid green eyes, and long dark hair. "What can I help ye with, lass?" Concerned yet understanding she wasn't home, she asked if she could be helped to find a few plain dresses and perhaps some new Mary Janes. "Of course, lass. Right here, you see. Potato sack dresses, dyed plain grey. Perfect for a slim woman your size, or anyone who dares to wear such an unflattering piece." Gee, thanks, she thought, not for her. But as she turned to leave, the unconventional-looking woman sighed and said she could show her additional choices.

Venturing behind a curtain in the back for a moment, the woman brought out more shapely dress options in what looked like black silk. "Fine customers only, these here are two hundred shekels each. No stealing these, they're kept safe from common folk."

Peering into her bag, she had what looked like a few thousand sickle-coined shekels left. Violet asked if she would accept only a meager one hundred fifty from a woman such as herself.

Scoffing, the woman replied that such words ought be left as thoughts and not spoken. She suggested a trade, stating that she could keep her coins in exchange for a favor.

"What sort of favor might that be, shopkeeper?" she asked.

She explained that she needed help reading a passage from her *Book of Forgetting*, that only two could read such words in a successful manner.

"What do you mean by that, ma'am? Can you not read your stories alone like I do?" Smirking, the woman replied that these aren't mere stories like you might find in a storybook.

"You can either give me two hundred shekels like I originally asked, or you can receive the silk gown for free in exchange for reading the passage with me," the shopkeeper said. Thinking about it for a moment, Violet decided that she would ponder it for a few hours and come back later.

After exiting the shop and spying a canteen up ahead, she chose to grab a quick lunch and think about the shopkeeper's proposed options. Sitting outside the canteen for a moment and unsure if the dress was truly necessary, as she was wearing a perfectly good one at this moment, she considered dismissing the encounter altogether. She chose not to do so, instead focusing on the shopkeeper's request. What could she have meant by no mere story? Is that not what each book was, potentially minus the texts that claim to be divine works? What was it with this strange world and its creatures? Mind-reading pedicab drivers, goblins as innkeepers, and unbelievably rude shopkeepers?

"Where am I?" Violet wondered. What had brought her to such a place, and why was she here? The reality of her situation dawned on her, and she briefly started to spiral and "split" into black-and-white thinking. "Oh no, in attempting to find a safe haven to read away from my sisters, I ended up in another world with seemingly no exit as I saw only blackness. How can I return to my world and my sad life? No, why would I want to? My siblings don't love me, my closest friend left me, and my parents are here no longer. I must make a name for myself, away from there," she thought to herself.

Still carrying her prized book, read many times until the spine began to crumble, she decided to read further. Engrossed in the words, she delayed lunch until the book was finished once again. Staring out the nearby window, she noticed that the sky had darkened slightly and that the lunch hour had turned to dinner. Several people passed by, ranging from normal in appearance to very abnormal.

She was famished, and decided to step into the diner for certain this time. Walking in, she was made to stand in line and ponder the menu. As she chose to forgo non-swimming meat long ago, her options were few. She could decide between soup of broccoli with crostini, a sandwich but with only tomatoes and mayo, a few scones in a dessert case window, and perhaps her choice of a few chunks of fish if she so desired. The line continued on, and since she was famished she chose a hunk of white fish along with the broccoli soup, a side of bread, and a blueberry lemon scone for afterwards. She scarfed it down quickly, feeling more satisfied than ever. She could think more soundly and in shades of grey now, still pondering what the green-eyed woman had meant. Realizing that the townsfolk might know more than she did, she returned to the ordering counter, saying "excuse me."

A brown-haired man with a kind face turned around, introduced himself "My name is Allen, it's nice to meet you," and asked how he could help such a lovely woman. Allen thought to himself that she was the most beautiful woman he had ever seen, far surpassing the beauty of any of the townsfolk.

She asked him what he knew of the sewing shop owner, and if he knew why she had such vivid irises. "My sweet thing...stay away from such a place if you have sense about yourself. She looks enticing and the wares are comfortable, but around these parts they speak whispers about her indulgence in the dark arts."

"The dark arts? What are those?" she asked.

He clarified, "Stay away, for good's sake. She reads the *Book of Forgetting*, and other tomes like it. We stay away, leaving the city for a nearby hamlet for our wares. You ought to do the same, if ye have wits about yourself. I've got to help others now, dear. But if you need me, come back and ask for me. Maybe we'll meet again sometime, and I'll suggest a stroll one twilight." He offered to help the next in line, forcing her to turn her thoughts elsewhere.

Could something seemingly intended to help one forget truly harm that much? She wished she could forget, or that none of these things ever happened to begin with. The pain of her existence always weighed on her heavily, and even when she smiled, a deep sadness lurked beneath. Sometimes she felt it would have been easier to have never been born, but she would never truly ask for that.

Why remember those who have hurt her? What could her memories help? For now, she intended to do as Allen said. Perhaps she would venture back one evening, as he suggested. She could see herself gleeful with such a kind-faced man, and felt that he was a more noble man than Lysander was after just that one encounter. Although she had never had romantic feelings towards Lysander, she often wondered if that feeling wasn't mutual. When he first started to grow feelings for another woman, he said something very strange that still stuck with her. "Meet me in front of the woods in twenty years, Violet. Wherever we have been, no matter if we are married, I want to see you in twenty years. Perhaps things could be different then." However, she knew his thought came from a place of idiocy and chose to not associate with him further. This led to a mutual dislike, and he never sought her out again. Although she some-times pondered what could be if she were to take him up on the encounter after two decades, she knew it was not what was best for her and tried to keep that thought out of her mind.

Returning to the inn with her hunger satisfied, she was determined to return to Allen the following day for that stroll. After a night filled with dreams of Allen and the barnman, she woke up in a pleasurable state for once. She intended to find food to break the fast, and a place to occupy her time for the day. Perhaps she would lose her prudishness and venture into a bar without taking any sips, or kiss the canteen server under the cover of shadow today. She was still determined to keep away from the green-eyed woman, although she didn't understand the start of what dark arts or forgetting meant.

She took a walk around the city, up and down streets and around the castle with its many turrets. After feeling a constant draw to the green-eyed woman's shop and her promise of the luscious dress in exchange for a favor, she hurried back to the shop, determined not to let Allen see her. Ignoring the small voice inside her head that warned her against it, she walked back inside.

The shopkeeper said, "I knew you'd stop in today. My name is Alice, pleasure to have your acquaintance. Now about my book..."

Violet was still hesitant, although drawn to make this trade. After much consideration, she asked what sort of book this was and what exactly was meant by forgetting.

"Dearest, I know what troubles you and that you wish to not remember. You mean to stay in this land, although you find it strange, and you want to move past the pain caused by a loveless upbringing. Isn't that right?"

Concerned about how much this woman was like Kazuki but in a much more forceful way, Violet asked how she knew that. "It's all in a book, sister to this one.

Now let's read this passage in my back room. Your memories will be how you wish them to be, and you will be better off. Let's be quick, and you won't regret your decision." Alice smiled at her.

"Why do you need my help?" Violet asked.

"Oh, sweet thing. I don't. I just know you need to read this, and I want to participate. I have work to do as well, and two voices make the effects stronger. Okay now? Let's do this before you think yourself out of it."

Alarm bells began tolling louder in her brain, but she thought back to Kazuki's words about how she had to meet someone. Might that be Alice, who could help her through her pain? Should she go through with this? "What will happen to my memories? Why do I need to read the words you want me to? What is this book?"

Alice became impatient, grabbed her right arm, and began to drag her into the back of her shop. She handed her a glass filled with liquid, and begged her to drink. "It'll help this go smoothly," she said.

Although her brain was urging her not to, Violet drank the whole glass in one chug, and returned it to Alice. Her vision blurred, but she felt calmer, if a bit unsteady, and stopped hearing the bells in her head.

Alice held the book out to her and pointed to a passage. The words began to levitate off the page, as if possessed by a force not of the world she came from. Violet read the words aloud, backed by Alice's voice, and once the words were said, everything went black. After some amount of time, she awoke. She was still in the shop's backroom, and Alice was standing over her.

"What happened to me?" Violet asked her.

Alice cackled and reminded Violet that she had gone through with what was asked. Then, she handed her the silk dress she liked and told her to be gone.

Unsure of what day or time it was but only knowing she needed to see Allen, Violet returned to the inn. The goblin man asked her if she would like to extend her stay, as she was supposed to have checked out this morning. She had all of her wares on her, so he had nothing to clear out.

Confused, she explained that she had only rested her head for two nights. He explained that she must be mistaken and that she had best be gone, or pay for another night. He tossed her a bag and said "for your dress in your arms."

She asked for a place to change, and he offered her the linen closet with a look of irritation. She removed her current dress and quickly replaced it with that of black silk. Placing her old dress, cloak, hat, book, and coins in the bag, she threw it over her shoulder and hurried back to the canteen, dressed in luxurious, fine silk. She entered the canteen and got in line, determined to speak to Allen again. When she got to the front of the line, she ordered the daily special: a house salad with scallops and raw yellow onions. She was feeling flirty and, batting her eyelashes, she told the fine young man that she would love to see him after his shift. She added that she would wait for him until he could see her after her meal.

She found a table with a single chair in the corner,

sat down with her large salad, and ate. After finishing her meal, she pulled her book back out. She got to chapter three, and Allen leaned over her.

"Time to close up shop. Nice dress, would you like to take that stroll I offered?" He held out his hand to her, and she took her bag and adjusted it so that it wouldn't bump him. They left the city gates and walked along a nearby stream complete with a swimming duck, and Allen felt the need to ask her about the black dress. "Where did you get that? Please don't tell me you went back to the witch's shop."

Perplexed, she asked, "What witch?"

Allen felt extremely concerned for her sanity at this point, and had to break it down step by step. He recounted, "Alice, the witch! Did the spellbook not give it away? I told you we go into the hamlet for our wares for a reason. She's not one to be messed with."

She had to back up a step. "After seeing the goblin innkeepers, I thought such striking eyes were normal in this world! Where I come from, Alice is only a name for elderly women and the night dwellers spoken of in myths. I should've paid more attention to that."

Despite her confusion and his concern for her well-being, Allen leaned in towards her and gently touched her cheek with his thumb. All smiles, he told her that she was "the most beautiful woman who has ever visited the canteen" and that he was very lucky to have met her. He kissed her briefly, just a brush of his lips against hers, and she returned to the inn alone for another night's stay.

The next morning, still remembering her past and starting to feel remorse for her encounter with Alice, she decided to return home to Circa. It was Sunday, and while Violet normally sat in the back row of her small church alone, she enjoyed spending time with the Lord despite her ever-present, melancholic, deeply rooted sadness-induced agnosticism. She hoped to return to her church just once, even if she knew her sisters would continue to spite her by not sitting with her. During church, her sisters always sat as far away from her as possible, generally near the front, as if to make Violet feel less than.

Sitting up in bed, she wondered why the room was still dark, unsure if she had risen before the sun. Shaking her head, knowing she occasionally woke up before six in the morning, she pulled on her cloak and boots, then padded down the stairs. As she cracked open the door to the inn, she immediately knew something was wrong. It appeared to be daylight hours, but a deep purple filled the sky, and the sun had barely started to make its appearance. She had never seen a purple sunrise, only sunset, and others nearby seemed to be concerned as well. Looking around, she noticed many others chattering to those next to them, some even pointing their fingers up to the deep violet, reminiscent of her name. After the moment of initial shock had passed, Kazuki again appeared and offered a ride.

Ever wise, Kazuki merely said, "It is what was meant to happen" when she asked about the sky's purple hue and didn't comment further when she asked if he knew what had happened. He wouldn't elaborate when pressed further, but Violet knew to trust what he said. When he got her back to where the light previously shimmered between the trees, nothing but the blackness she previously noticed remained.

She tried to push through, beginning to pound on the wall of blackness. As she was growing frustrated and upset, Alice showed up. "Well, well, well," she said. "Look who we have here. What do you think the spell of forgetting did, my dear? You hoped you might forget your past, but your past has now been forgotten from this world. You wanted to forget your sisters, but now the portal to everyone you've ever known is gone. Access to your village has been destroyed, and your whole world might as well have been destroyed with it. Thank you by the way, I had a vendetta against them. But that's a story for another day, or never...It's awfully funny that you thought you couldn't turn back before, but you didn't try," then she winked. She continued, "Your past is dead to you but you won't forget. Best be gone from here and move on, shoo now!" She started shoo-gesturing for her to walk away.

Violet did not understand, but Alice reminded her that she told her that her memories would be "how she wished them to be." Violet wished for them to be gone, but she guessed the access to the existence of the physicality of her memories was gone even if her memories remained. Alice said "You'll understand someday, Violet," and then disappeared as if she was never there.

Kazuki seemed to have heard this exchange, so he

apologized on behalf of Alice. There wasn't much that could be done now, though. Despite wishing for almost exactly this, she grew greatly upset that her sisters and Lysander were gone, and she didn't know what to do. She even began to miss her irritating neighbor Andrew, whom she always tried to avoid. For now, she decided to head back to Greensfeld. Although she didn't want to, she had better get on with her life until she could find a way to restore the portal—if such a thing was even possible.

"Kazuki?" she asked, and as he understood her thoughts without her vocalizing them, they were off. Realizing he had more insight to this strange world than she did, she paused for a moment before asking him why the sun wasn't rising. Several hours had passed since starting their journey, and the sky maintained its seemingly bewitched shade of purple.

"I don't know, Violet. And that is saying something. I truly don't know what could cause such an occurrence, but it's concerning to myself as well. Don't think otherwise, even if I'm not reactive. However, I feel deeply inside myself that this event was meant to occur."

The return journey felt faster than the way back to the forest. Soon, she was checking in at the inn again. The innkeeper remarked on the sky, asking what she thought of it, although the sky was returning to the deep black of night. Sighing, she ignored his remark and continued on to her room. She thought to herself that she needed to find a more permanent living situation, though.

The next morning, with no sun in sight, she took a stroll through the city streets and alleys. Upon passing the green-eyed woman's store, she noticed that it was boarded up and closed. How would she ever find another portal to her home world without Alice? Her ever-present sadness made her want to collapse at this point, so she returned to the inn and pulled the bed covers over her head and cried. She felt like no matter what she did, she was doing it wrong. She felt like a burden on the world, and she started to feel this was becoming accurate instead of just the dark thoughts that had haunted her throughout her life.

As the days passed and she sank deeper into depression, she had a fitful nightmare. She couldn't sleep because she heard her sisters calling out to her. While she knew it was only her imagination and that they would not care to attempt to reach her even if they could, she knew they were still there, even if she couldn't access them. She started to feel that her life was meant to be miserable, and she would have been better off suffering as the youngest sibling than trying to escape her reality. The thought was breaking her. She had wanted to forget them, not for them to be forgotten to this world. She decided that she needed to do something to try to restore access to her home world and find Alice so that she could confront her.

One day, amidst the monotony, Kazuki asked to show Violet something unique that might help get her mind off of her misery for a short period of time—the bridge to nowhere. Although it had seemingly no purpose, just off the northern coast was a wooden plank suspension boardwalk that led nowhere. Instead, it protruded into the deep blue ocean and welcomed mildly crashing waves before circling back around, ending a few miles off from where it started. Kazuki warned Violet that it would be an interesting yet nearly pointless journey, but she expressed her gratitude for the support. Kazuki pulled up his pedicab, and Violet said "thank you" as she got in. They set off. As they approached the bridge, Violet let out an audible sound of amazement. It truly was a drawbridge off into the distance, with no end in sight. Kazuki and Violet set off towards the sea, and at one point, the planks drifted under the water, dilapidated. A small crowd of visitors had gathered, debating whether to turn back or continue on their circular journey. Violet said, "come on," and disembarked the pedicab before proceeding to drag it toward the water. They engaged in what they would later think of as "bridge swimming." They pulled the pedicab as they swam across the gap, before embarking on their journey again.

"Ah, spontaneous bridge swimming. What a marvel, Violet," Kazuki stated, always filled with zaniness. They eventually reached the place where the bridge curved back to shore, far out into the sea with no end of the water in sight. Turning around, Violet was grateful to have spent a few hours engaged in spontaneity and now felt a stronger bond with her strange companion, starting to see him as more of a friend. They followed the rest of the bridge to nowhere before Kazuki dropped

Violet off and pedaled off to wherever he went at night. Despite having spoken to Kazuki for hours on multiple occasions, she hadn't thought to ask the mysterious empath a single question about his personal life.

The following day, as she couldn't think of anything else to do, she decided to seek solace in a new book or two. Wandering around the streets of the city, she came across a small library hidden off the corner of a side street in a neglected part of the city. After taking a deep breath, she went inside. She walked up and down the aisles, trying to find a text that might mention the *Book of Forgetting* and its capabilities. She thought that since the library was in an older part of the city, she might have luck. She soon found beaten up antique books in a back section and hoped they could provide valuable insight.

Walking to the back of the library, she spotted a man who looked familiar. It was the man who owned the barn that she had spent the night in! This couldn't be a coincidence, but she was not sure how she could speak to him without giving away her trespassing. She decided to pay him no mind for now, to focus, instead, on the task ahead of her, and to inspect each old book one by one. Dusting off the covers, she found three books in the section that may have information, all focused on the mythology of spellcasting and whether or not such a thing was real: *Arcane Truths*, *The Green Witch's Handbook*, and *The Spellbound*.

Finding a comfortable and plush leather chair, she decided to sit down. She indulged her curiosity and started poring over the first volume, but she couldn't find any information beyond the hypothetical. It was an intriguing read and got her out of her head, but it didn't help her quest to restore the portal.

Opening the second book, she saw the words "look beyond the lever" inscribed inside the front cover. Not knowing what was meant by that, she started reading. An occasional word was underlined or highlighted in deep orange, a strange pigment, but she didn't see any other information that could be deemed helpful. After finishing the second volume, the stranger from the barn sat down in a chair near her.

"Hello ma'am, my name is Felix. You seem familiar but I cannot put my finger on why. Have you been in this library before?"

Not wanting to blow her cover, she simply replied that he seemed familiar as well but that it was her first time in the library. Honest, but not completely. Continuing to focus on her reading, she kept pondering the *Book of Forgetting* and the Spell of Forgetting, as well as the inscribed words from the second volume. She continued reading, but nothing else stuck out. The library was set to close as the sky grew black, so she checked out all three books and returned to the inn. She could continue thinking once she was alone again and in the comforts of her rented and temporary bed. Finding more permanent lodging still occupied her thought, but was not something she could dwell on presently. After reading through the two remaining books, she found nothing helpful and decided to turn in for the night.

The next morning, feeling well-rested despite the

pressure to find a solution, she returned to the library. "Look behind the lever, look behind the lever, look behind the lever" she repeated in her mind. But what could that mean? She continued looking around the store for any other tomes that could be considered helpful and was about to ask the short-statured young woman at the receptionist's desk if there was another library or bookstore in the city or perhaps a neighboring town. Just as she started to walk towards her, she noticed a book seemingly inconspicuously placed at a strange angle high up on a shelf against the back left corner of the library. She approached it, looked both ways, and assuming this might be the lever mentioned, pulled the book off the shelf. The bookcase moved away, opening a doorway to a tunnel that went down into darkness. Determined, she walked into the tunnel, and the bookcase slid back into place.

CHAPTER 3

The tunnel was damp and smelled of mildew, and utter blackness surrounded her. The tunnel could have been endless. "It would have been nice to have brought some flint and tinder to start a fire, or perhaps a lit torch," she thought to herself. Feeling with her hands along the wall, she took slow and steady steps. A divot in the flooring caused her to stumble, but she eventually saw a small crack of purple-tinted light up ahead on the left path of a fork in the tunnel. She saw her life laid out before her, with a fork diverging into two paths: one towards the light and another towards darkness. She thought back to something her mother once told her, that the dark path doesn't lead to happiness. She was always told it would lead to destruction. Approaching quietly and cautiously, she arrived at the source of the small crack of light: what appeared to be the back of a cellar door. Thinking for a moment, she slid open the cellar door.

Grateful to not be seen, she exited the chamber and closed the door. She was unsure of the point of the tunnel, as it only took her from within the library to just outside the castle. Most might just assume it was the entrance to one of the castle's many wine cellars and pay it no mind. Feeling like the endeavor was a waste of time, she started walking back to the main entrance of the library. Clearly there was something behind a lever, but maybe not that lever.

After rereading the same books as before, she encountered the farmer again. He asked her if she had any experience as a stable hand, as he was looking for a caregiver for his chickens and she seemed capable enough to fill that role. She decided to go along with it, grabbed her bag from the inn, and carted along to the hamlet, called Amberlet, with the farmer.

When they got to the farm, she was given a stall in the barn for the time being. He placed a small cot there to act as a temporary bed. She explored the chicken farm, noticing that the farmhouse and chicken coop were very far from the dilapidated barn. But any accommodations were better than no accommodations, and she had already stayed here for free one night anyway.

Laying on her cot, she thought back to one of her most vivid childhood memories. She was a young girl, perhaps five or six years old, and she and her father were taking a walk near their home. Two young women were walking in the opposite direction holding hands, and her father had covered Violet's eyes as if it was wrong to love the same sex. Since she had known from a young age that she liked both men and women, this memory had always stuck with her.

A few weeks later, she decided to return to the library tunnel and, against her mother's guidance, see where the dark path led. She walked along the path, and it came to a door. The door had a crack beneath it, and she peeped under it. The door appeared to lead into the castle's private library, but it was locked, and she couldn't access it. Maybe she could acquire locksmithing tools to help her out, but she would have to return another time.

Thinking back to her time in Circa, the village where she had grown up, she realized that the most important lesson she had learned recently was not to count your chickens before they hatched. Even if something seemed certain, she could never predict what would happen. She thought she would be guaranteed safety with her friend if not her sisters, but she was tossed to the side, thrown into a world she would have never dreamed existed, and forced to forge her own path in life.

Getting back to Amberlet for the night, she took a different route and passed a small pond that she hadn't seen before. Off to the side of the lake was a short and frail gray-haired woman, who appeared to be talking to a goose. Knowing that the world couldn't get much stranger than she already thought it was, she approached the old woman and introduced herself. "I'm Violet Evans, a new farmhand at the nearby chicken farm. Who do I have the pleasure of speaking to?"

The old woman composed herself for a moment and looked behind herself briefly, as if nervous, and said "My name is Ruth. I live down the trail and around the bend. I often come to this pond to think, because I feel like my goose, Goosey, is the only being who understands me. She suffers from anxiety and prefers the pond to my home, you see, and we have conversations, Goosey and me."

Feeling a little concerned for Ruth's sanity, she wasn't quite sure how to respond. After a moment, she said that it must be nice to have the companionship of a non-judgmental creature and that she might have to talk to the goose as well.

Ruth laughed and asked if there was anything she could help her with. Not wanting to burden a woman she had just met, she started to return to the barn for the night.

Ruth called out to her "Dearie, no, I think I can help you. Come sit with Goosey and me and tell me what's on your mind."

She told her that she was trying to find a woman named Alice from the nearby city who had done something wrong to her, but Alice had disappeared, and, since she wasn't from the area, she didn't know where to look.

"Oh, I know Alice. She's not very nice, but we all know her. I used to be like her when I was younger. I'll help you find her if you'll do me a favor." A favor? Oh no, what could she be getting herself into by offering favors to those she doesn't know well?

"Not a big favor, I'm just weary and don't walk as well as I used to, so I avoid it if I can help it. Get me a slice of cake from the bakery in Greensfeld, and we'll talk. I know Alice, and you have my word that I know where she is if she doesn't want to be found by someone not well acquainted with her." Feeling confused and concerned, Violet cocked her head to the side and asked her to elaborate. "I was a witch, a good, white witch, when I was your age. We all reported to Alice, queen of the witches, whether we were a white witch, also known as a green witch, or a black witch. Alice is a black witch, the kind to avoid. I know where the witches are. I'll trade my knowledge for some brown butter cake from Bad Cakes." Violet inquired as to how she would find her. "You'll find me if you find the goose," was all Ruth felt to clarify.

"Brown butter cake, brown butter cake," Violet muttered to herself as she walked back to the barn for the night. It was too late to acquire the cake, so she thought it best to just go to bed.

The next day, Violet went to Felix and asked for a bobby pin or two to keep her hair pinned back. He gave her a jar full and said that now was as good of time as any to introduce her to the chickens. Violet followed behind him as they walked to the chicken coop, and she was extremely surprised when she laid her eyes on a coop full of female blue chickens. She had never seen or heard of a chicken that wasn't white, brown, or possibly black or grey.

"Impressive, don't you say? I bred them myself! It takes a strong line of black and splash genetics to produce blue hens, and I've kept this going for a few generations now. Best in town, might even take them to show," he said.

That afternoon, as the ever-dark tinted the sky, Violet had just stopped by the barn to grab her brown satchel, complete with her jar of bobby pins, when she ran into Kazuki. "Kazuki, perfect timing! Can you take me into the city for a few hours? I'm in need of some brown butter cake from Bad Cakes."

He responded, "Bad Cakes? Why would you want to go there? It's run by a kitchen full of talking cats and headed up by a warlock. Sure, the cakes are good, but they infuse the sugar with witchcraft, so it's mainly only frequented by witches of both varieties, wizards and warlocks, the occasional mage, and unsuspecting humans."

Momentarily confused as to why the white witch would suggest she go there, she asked "What's wrong with the cakery besides that it's run by magical beings? Is the food bad? The magical sugar can't be bad for you, right?"

Kazuki told her that she should climb in the pedicab and that he could explain on the way. Once she climbed aboard, he clarified that there's not necessarily anything wrong with the magic-infused sugar, but it helps magical creatures ground themselves if they're able to burn off some magic, and one way of doing so was to infuse their magic into foods such as sugar. That way, they can avoid a magical burnout and consume the magic later when feeling worn out and in need of a rush.

Still confused, she felt the need to clarify. "Does it affect humans?"

Kazuki raised his right eyebrow and told her "No, but that's irrelevant anyway. Enough for now."

Violet wasn't sure what he meant by that but trusted his judgment. They rode on in silence, and the ever-dark started to turn into the black of night, but they pulled up to Bad Cakes as the last purple tinge of the day faded away to black. She pulled open the door, and a bell strung to the handle started to jingle, marking her entrance. She walked up to the counter and noted that, indeed, the cakery was run by talking cats. A black fuzzy, small-ish cat was manning the shekel exchange box, sitting on top of a wooden stool.

"Meow and welcome, how can I help you this evening?" Violet was somewhat in shock, but responded that she needed three slices of brown butter cake as quickly as cattingly possible.

"Meow," said the cat. She grabbed the three slices of cake, each bagged separately in wax paper and brown paper wrap on the outside, and asked how much it would cost for all three.

He said "twenty shekels from your pocket, ma'am."

She exchanged her shekels for the cake slices, carefully arranged them in her bag beside the jar of bobby pins, and walked back outside to Kazuki. "I understand that nightfall is quickly approaching, but can we make another stop before we head home? Also, where is home for you, sir?"

He laughed and said that his only intention was to make those around him happy, but "we have time for another stop tonight." She asked if they could swing by the library, as she had something she needed to do rather quickly. He pedaled them to the library, and she disembarked. "Twenty minutes until they close, Violet. Better be quick!"

She went back inside, seeing Allen, the man she had begun to grow deep-rooted feelings for. Winking, she continued to the back of the store, looking both ways before activating the secret lever. Accessing the tunnel again, with a jar full of bobby pins "for her hair" in her pocket, she felt determined. Unsure how to pick the lock, she believed in herself and felt she could do it if she set her mind to it. Approaching the locked door yet again, she knelt on the ground with her right knee as one does in a church and began wiggling her bobby pin in the lock. It didn't appear to have enough momentum on its own, so she added a separate bobby pin to the mix. Using both hands and a variety of movements with her fingers, she managed to open the lock after approximately ten minutes.

Saying a silent prayer, she turned the handle and pulled open the door. Thankfully, the castle's private library was empty now with no sign of that changing. She wondered whether the library would have a book that referenced the *Book of Forgetting* or Spell of Forgetting. "Hmm," she thought to herself. Careful not to make a sound or disturb the quiet, she marveled at the scenery of the library. Inhaling through her nose briefly, she took in the scent of a rarely-disturbed collection of antique, dusty books. It had a much different scent than that of the main library she was just in. Realizing Kazuki would soon grow suspicious and that she would like to avoid that if at all possible, she quickly walked to the far corner of the library as she noticed maroon velvet drapes covering one particular bookcase. After displacing the drapes and inspecting the now exposed shelf, she noticed that it mainly included what appeared to be journals and diaries of various kinds. However, on the bottom shelf on the far right was a hardcover book, the spine of which was labeled *The Cost to Pay to Forget*. With her time running out, she decided to take that book for now and return to Kazuki before he grew wary. She secured the book in her bag before carefully replacing the curtain. Ensuring the door to the castle library was locked upon her exit, she chose to leave through the cellar door in case the library was closed. Pondering a potential excuse and thinking of none that were good, she carefully cracked the cellar door and looked to see if she was alone. She didn't hear a footstep and didn't see even a mouse, so she quietly and slowly opened the cellar door. Looking left and right, she carefully put the door back into position and started to walk to the front of the library that she came from.

However, as she picked up pace and headed towards the library, Allen came around a corner and called out "Hello, Violet!"

Not intending to cause a scene, she replied "Hello Allen, good evening," and continued walking to where she was sure Kazuki was impatiently waiting. Glancing back, Allen appeared like he wanted to continue the conversation, but he seemingly decided against it, as he didn't utter another syllable. "I'll see you again soon, Allen," she half-shouted with what she hoped was a kind tone. Rounding the side of the library, she spotted Kazuki and stated, "Great to see you, let's head back now." Knowing she was acting mildly suspicious, she observed Kazuki's behavior to see if he had caught on. He raised his left eyebrow at her this time, but said nothing. She climbed aboard and ate her cake while he pedaled her back to Amberlet. Kazuki also told her that he ate his slice of brown butter cake while she was in the library, and that it was the best he'd ever had.

When they neared the hamlet and she had eaten the last morsel of her cake slice, she asked Kazuki if he knew where to find Ruth and Goosey. "Are they always near the pond?" she asked. He wasn't sure but offered to drop her off near the pond regardless. They headed that way, and she disembarked, calling out "Ruth!" despite the hour of night.

There was no sign of Ruth, but Goosey let out a loud and nasal "honk." Startled, Violet froze up for a moment, not expecting the honk of a goose. When she opened her eyes, she noticed that Goosey was up in a tree branch far off the ground.

"Ah, lesser magic," Ruth said as she approached.

Unsure of what she meant, Violet asked, "What do you mean?"

Ruth responded that when Violet was startled, she froze up and blew Goosey into the tree.

Believing there was no way such a thing was possible, Violet stated, "But geese can fly, I didn't do anything to harm this goose despite the fright she caused me."

Ruth countered, "But you did indeed. Goosey can't fly. She has been that way for as long as I have known her. In spite of this, your mother was a witch, Violet. In fact, she was Alice's much younger sister. You're a white witch like I am. I just thought it best to wait until you came to that conclusion yourself."

Bewildered, Violet took a step back. "I brought the cake you requested. The cakery was a little different from what I was expecting, but I brought you a brown butter cake. I was told they imbue the sugar with magic, yes?" She then reached into her satchel and pulled out the cake slice, holding it out to her. Ruth bowed as a sign of thanks, and then took the cake slice from her hand. Grabbing what appeared to be a fork but made out of bark, she sat on the grass and began to eat. "What do you mean, my mother was Alice's sister? I feel as if I would have known I had an evil witch in my lineage. Will I become like her if left unchecked?" she said, her voice filled with worry.

"Sit, dearest. Goosey will have to be stuck in that tree a while longer, poor thing. I need to take a moment to rest with this cake, and you're much too short to reach the high branch you blew her up onto." Ruth continued eating while Violet stared up at the goose and wondered how a shimmer between two tree branches led to all of this. Taking several minutes to think over the events that led up to her leaving her village and everything that transpired afterward, she became mystified.

"Ruth, if I'm a witch—and Alice's niece at that—is that why Alice closed off the portal to my home world?" Ruth, still eating, held up her index finger to her mouth, intending to keep Violet in the dark a moment longer. Several moments later, Ruth said that she needed to fetch her dear goose from the tree before continuing this conversation. Violet, still sitting as she had while Ruth ate her slice of cake, looked up at Ruth, who gently used the wind to bring Goosey down into her arms and set her on the ground.

Ruth took a deep breath, in and out, and then began again, "There are two ways witches can gain their powers. You can either learn them yourself through dark arts, or you can be born to a bloodline that carries magical powers. Once a person gains magical powers, all of their direct descendants will as well. However, only the first generation dark witch, also known as black witch, or warlock if they are a man, will possess dark magic. All future generations become white witches, also known as green witches due to their connection to the earth, or wizards, depending on their sex. White witches can become dark witches if they so choose, but that is a choice. Dark witches are made, not born."

Violet appeared visibly confused, so Ruth tried to break things down a bit better. "Because you come from a bloodline of witches, you were born a white witch. I'm a white witch, just like you, but I mentioned that earlier. In my twenties, I made the journey to Witch Island intending to become a dark witch like Alice. I studied the art for several years, but decided to back away before I ever cast a dark spell myself. My white witch nature is what differentiates me from Alice. As for your mother, I can't say whether she was a white or black witch since that isn't my story to tell, but I can confirm that your mother was indeed a witch. You come from a long line of witches on your mother's side. Your mother's line has been considered royalty among witchkind and has been entirely pure. Your father's side, however, had a few mortals diluting the bloodline."

Surprised, Violet took a moment to compose herself before she replied, "Well how do I find her? Where can Alice be found?"

Ruth responded, "I mentioned Witch Island earlier, and thank you again for the brown butter cake. Alice is the Queen of the Witches and makes her home on Witch Island. On the far side of the island stands a tall, black castle. Alice can be found there, but I'm not sure she'll speak to you."

Feeling as if Ruth wasn't getting to the point fast enough, Violet asked "But how can I get to Witch Island? Where is it? How far off the coast is it? Where even is the coast?"

Remembering that Violet wasn't from here originally, Ruth stated "Witch Island is several miles off the west coast of the continent. The waters are choppy and oft filled with pirates. If you're going to go to the island, you'll need to be prepared for the journey. The coast is not far from here, perhaps a 12 hour journey by horse or pedicab. Much longer if you walk, I would imagine a day or two. Perhaps it would help if I explain our geography, knowing that you're not familiar with or from our world?"

After her discussion with Ruth and Goosey, Violet returned to the chicken farm, fed the chickens, and laid down to read the book she pilfered from the castle's library. However, the pages were mostly blank, with no reasonable explanation as to why. One thing stuck out to her, though: the prophecy. Looking back on when she had first crossed through the portal, she remembered the crow cawing out:

"Hear ye, heed ye, the foolish deed,
Of heart unwise and reckless need.
The sun begins, but shall not stay,
No noontime high in the month of May,
And all the world in twilight lay."

After thinking things through more clearly, she began to realize that she was the "unwise" spoken of in the crow's prophecy.

As Violet was preparing to leave, Allen unexpectedly appeared at the chicken farm. His demeanor was warm and inviting as he asked if she would accompany him on another date. Together, they strolled away from the farm, the cool evening air surrounding them despite the ever-dark.

Allen, with sincerity in his voice, spoke: "I know it is

early on, but when you know, you know. I can't help but mention that I love you, Violet." His confession caught her by surprise but also filled her with a warmth she hadn't anticipated. He continued, proposing something unconventional yet heartfelt, "Would you consider sharing my tenement house with me? It might not be traditional, but I feel we will need each other's support for the journeys ahead."

Curious and invested, Violet agreed to move in together and then asked Allen to share more about his past. He relayed a story about losing his father at a young age. He had no siblings and no distant family that he was aware of, so he was very close with his mother. Much like himself, she held the belief that one does not remarry after losing a spouse, a sentiment Violet found herself agreeing with. Despite the loss, Allen described how his mother had found a career as a teacher, which brought joy and stability into their lives.

"I hope you will meet her someday," he said to Violet. "I think you would really like her." Continuing to tell Violet about himself, "I am religious," Allen admitted, "but not devoutly so." His moderate approach to faith resonated with Violet, and she nodded in agreement.

She responded, "I am religious, but more in a broad sense, and I am transparently very agnostic despite my religious beliefs. I know that may sound confusing." He shook his head and said that Violet was very charming just the way she was. Their shared values laid a strong foundation for the relationship they were beginning to build.

As the ever-dark turned to night, Violet felt a growing sense of comfort and connection with Allen. His openness and honesty were qualities that she deeply appreciated. She realized that, though their journey together was just starting, it held the promise of a shared life together. Kissing Allen briefly, she was becoming very hopeful for what could happen in the future, despite the many burdens she shouldered each day.

CHAPTER 4

The following morning, Violet moved her few belongings into Allen's home. She was greeted at the door with the smell of freshly brewed peppermint tea, and Allen asked her what she thought of their place. "It's perfect for the two of us. I only hope that you won't grow sick of me," she replied.

Later that afternoon, Allen went to work at the canteen, and Violet chose to venture to Witch Island and go after Alice. After a brief search, Kazuki was nowhere to be found, so she rented a tricycle in the hamlet. After an uncomfortable journey, she arrived at the coast. There were a few rowboats tied to the shore, and she grabbed one, thinking to herself that this was too easy. After resting for a moment, she began to row in a westerly direction.

She arrived at Witch Island, her heart pounding with a mixture of apprehension and curiosity as her eyes took in the eerie sight. As the rowboat approached the island's fog-shrouded shore, a plethora of odors in the heavy, damp air engulfed Violet's senses. The large, literal board with its ominous message "Unwelcome to Witch Island, now be gone!" loomed, a stark contrast to the dark, yet natural beauty of the island.

The island itself appeared to be a place lost to the world, enveloped in an oppressive silence broken only by the rustling of the heavy tree cover and the cawing of distant crows. The trees looked much different than the stone pines she was familiar with, standing tall and gnarled. The air was thick with the pungent scent of decay: a heady mix of dead roses, musty books, and woody mushrooms clung to every breath. While she did not believe witches were real before passing through the portal, this was what she imagined a dwelling for witches would be like.

As she stepped onto the shore, a shiver ran down her spine, along with the feeling of being watched. The ground beneath her feet was damp and spongy, like rotten moss, as though the island clung to her with every step. The only sound was the soft lapping of water against the boat, and the distant cry of a bird of prey.

Violet realized that finding Alice on this foreboding island was not going to be an easy task. The dense fog seemed to swallow up any sense of direction, and the heavy tree cover reduced visibility to no more than a few feet ahead. Every squelching step she took seemed to echo through the oppressive silence, like a ripple in a stagnant pool. Taking glances behind her, she felt like she was being watched, but she wasn't sure by what or whom.

She couldn't shake the feeling that she was being drawn deeper into the heart of darkness, and she wondered if she would ever find Alice amidst the eerie and unsettling landscape. In spite of this, she continued walking forward, determined to find the answer to her predicament. She continued on, and the terrain started to turn into a swamp, with a strong sulphuric odor that reminded her of the waste she collected from the chicken farm. Up ahead, she noticed a small hut with greyish-black smoke swirling up out of the small chimney on the right side of the roof. Unsure of whether or not to approach the hut, she took a moment to compose herself. Glancing down, she noticed a small scrap of paper on the ground. Curious, she picked it up, thinking "What is this?" It appeared to be a poem, reading:

"Allergies!

Then I sneeze.

Cough and hack,

And then I wheeze."

— El Hoffman

Not sure what that had to do with anything or what the point of that was, she folded up the scrap of paper and put it in her pocket to inspect again later. That was entertaining enough for the moment, but now she needed to keep moving.

As she continued to walk, she saw a pointy hat strewn on the right side of the path, and on the left side was a large meadow spread out before her, but filled with red toadstools as far as the eye could see. It truly looked like an island made for witches, but she wasn't quite sure where she fit in yet. New to being a witch, she pondered whether or not she fit in on the island or in the magical world as a whole, or if she was better off back in her village despite her misery. Recalling her nightmare, she wondered if she would ever fit in back home—or truly belong anywhere. As she walked further, she saw the outline of what appeared to be Alice's black castle hazed in the distance, and she began to mentally prepare herself for what would most likely be a difficult conversation. She began to regret not inviting Allen or Ruth along, but she knew she was strong and resilient on her own despite her sadness.

Continuing on the path, she heard cackling in the distance, coming from the direction of the castle. Knowing that witches cackle from her world's tales of folklore, she wasn't terribly concerned, but she realized she needed to read the book she stole before talking to Alice. She found a quiet toadstool large enough to sit on under a tree and briefly felt nostalgic for the log she often read on in the woods back home. She pulled *The Cost to Pay to Forget* out of her satchel. Realizing she had forgotten to ask Ruth about it before departing, she hoped she would be able to understand enough without the woman who had essentially become her mentor. After opening the book, she noticed what appeared to be journal entries discussing memory loss through various means, ranging from spells to illnesses, and the implications of information being forgotten. While most of the information was not immediately helpful, it did address potential causes for loss of memory late in life which could prove useful eventually. Twenty or so pages in, she read this passage:

"The spell of forgetting:

It is I, to forget, this world undone

It is from this

World forgoes this for now

Unto this, it is done"

Not recognizing this passage from what she had read with Alice, she still didn't understand why reading with Alice caused the portal between her world and this one to close. She wondered if a later passage might give more helpful information so she continued reading. Later in the book, there was a passage that explained that the majority of the *Book of Forgetting* was written in an English-like old language, only spoken by black witches, so she would've only been reading vowel and consonant sounds when she was with Alice. That helped her understand why she didn't quite understand what was happening, but even in English, the words didn't make much sense. She thought that perhaps it's more about the way the words are said and the meaning behind them together than the meaning of the actual words individually—like how a whole is worth more than the sum of its parts added together.

She shook her head and skimmed through passages about memory loss due to trauma and more passages about illness and old age before landing on a passage that was exactly what she had needed. "When spoken aloud by a black witch or in combination with multiple witches, spells have the intended effect that the witch perceives within a spectrum of perceived meaning, rather than what the words say verbatim. This means that although spells might collectively serve a purpose, the specific spell's effects are up to the black witch reading them." After reading that passage, she continued skimming and noticed another: "In the world of magic, spells are not solely defined by the words spoken but are deeply intertwined with the intentions of the caster and the interpretation of the magic itself. Each spell holds a spectrum of potential meanings and effects, and it is ultimately up to the practitioner, known as the black witch, to channel their intent and determine the specific outcome. For example, a single spell may hold the power to induce memory loss, but its exact manifestation—whether it erases specific memories, implants false ones, or prevents access to the people or place involved in the memories—is determined by the intention and focus of the caster. This dynamic interplay between intent and interpretation allows for a rich and nuanced practice of magic, where the nuances of language and the subtleties of intention shape the very fabric of reality." After both of these, she better understood that spells could be used for multiple purposes and not always for the same thing. While the Spell of Forgetting was explained in a way that made her feel like she would forget about her past and the pain it caused her, Alice had wanted to close the portal and her intentions caused that to happen. Violet imagined that these were techniques Ruth had learned in her training but decided to never implement.

After skimming through the rest of the book, she didn't find any other pertinent information. Seeing a good opportunity to continue looking for Alice, she continued walking towards the hazy outline of the castle.

After several more minutes of walking, she heard Ruth's voice whisper-shouting, "Violet!" Bewildered, she turned toward her voice and asked why she followed her to Witch Island. She responded, "I realized you need my help, Alice is a tough egg to crack."

Nervous, Violet admitted she didn't feel ready for the confrontation. "The more I learn of her, the more it feels that she can't be defeated," she said to Ruth.

Ruth replied, "That's why I followed you, Violet. You can handle this, but you don't need to do it alone. I believe in you and you are stronger than you think. This is the right thing to do, even if I hoped Alice would change long before you were ever born."

Violet nodded and agreed, "She needs to be stopped, and I can't turn back now."

Ruth painted a smile on her face that didn't feel entirely genuine and said "We'll confront her together," before looking away briefly with a pained look on her face. They continued walking and exchanged a cautious glance as they approached the imposing black castle, its ominous appearance growing larger with each step. The air grew colder, carrying an unnatural stillness that hinted at Alice's presence. Although Ruth navigated them towards the old servant's passage—a dark, narrow doorway hidden between bushes and beneath layers of overgrown ivy—they both knew their effort was likely in vain. "She knows we're here," Ruth muttered under her breath, her tone resigned. "She always knows."

Violet nodded, gripping her cloak tighter. The eerie silence of the servant's passage only heightened her unease. The dim, musty corridor snaked through the castle, climbing upward in a labyrinth of shadowy turns. But even within its concealed pathways, Violet couldn't shake the unsettling feeling of being watched. Ruth tried to reassure her with quiet whispers, though she didn't seem entirely convinced herself.

The castle, it seemed, was as much a part of Alice as her magic itself. The walls radiated a subtle hum of energy, as though the structure lived. Violet imagined the bricks reporting their every move as if made of eyes. Yet, no one stopped them. No servants scurried past, no distant footsteps echoed against the stone walls. It was as if the castle had been emptied deliberately, cleared for their audience with Alice.

Upwards they climbed, until they emerged onto the highest floor of the left turret—Alice's office, Ruth had confirmed in quiet tones. The heavy double doors to the office loomed before them, black and ornately carved, their intricate details contrasting with the emptiness they had witnessed moments earlier. Without warning, the doors creaked open of their own accord, revealing the shadowed interior beyond.

Ruth and Violet exchanged one last glance before

stepping inside, prepared to confront whatever Alice had in store for them.

After reaching Alice, Ruth and Violet were met with a loud cackle and a dark rumble of thunder from the distance. "Violet, Violet, Violet. You think to kill me? Try to kill me all you would like, but you can't open your pathetic little portal without shutting down the power source." She then pushed a large stream of air towards Violet, knocking her off her feet.

"What do you mean, *Aunt* Alice? What power source?"

Alice smirked, pushing another stream of air towards Violet, knocking her to the ground very quickly. "I'm a blood witch, dearie. Only one of our kind, or at least that's what I'll tell you. Fearing my death, I locked a few drops of my blood inside the magical power source in the Mountain Kingdom's Dark Valley within the Modern Realm. After my death, any spell of mine will hold as long as the power source does, but without the power source...there would be no veins of power. The choice is yours, dearest, but you won't get to the power source. Now get out of here!"

Suddenly, another gust of wind swept in accompanied with a flash of light. Pushed through a portal in Alice's wardrobe, Ruth and Violet found themselves back at the entrance to Witch Island, denoted by the sign "Unwelcome to Witch Island, now be gone!"

Leaving the island and its waters and returning to the mainland, Ruth and Violet noticed a horrific sight. A pedicab was strewn off the side of the path, smashed into an oak tree. As Violet approached with Ruth trailing behind her, they saw Kazuki lying off to the side, no longer of this world. Violet knew that Kazuki had long been using opium as she had noticed the smell and clouds of smoke, but as this world was different from her own she was never concerned. However, seeing him like this showed that he must have taken a turn for the worse. Devastated, Violet dropped to her knees and sobbed. Ruth knelt beside her, offering what little support she could in this devastating moment. Despite his words of encouragement and rides wherever she desired, Violet now felt that Kazuki, her enigmatic guide, was simply a product of her own perception, influenced by the intoxicating effects of drugs. Although she already chose to live a sober-minded life, in her tear-faced state, she vowed to never touch an addictive substance.

CHAPTER 5

"Ruth, what is the power source? What is a blood witch? I thought there were just white and black witches!" Violet spoke loudly enough that it could have been perceived as shouting, but she felt vexed.

Ruth replied, "I am not familiar with the power source, but I have suspicions about what she meant by that. As for blood witches, they are a far worse form of black witches. So terrible that they are rarely spoken of, and transparently, I try to forget that Alice deals in blood magic. I support blood oaths, but not spells cast with blood." Ruth began to feel upset at the reminder of Alice's true nature, as if there was something she wasn't telling Violet.

Violet continued asking Ruth questions, intending to learn more about what they were up against. "What do you think Alice meant about 'the Mountain Kingdom?' and the 'Modern Realm?' What are they?" Violet asked.

Sighing, Ruth stated that over the years she had heard rumors about a kingdom hidden in caves and an above-ground valley deep in the snowy Hyacinth mountains to the east. "The problem is that, Violet, no one has ventured into the mountains in decades. It's often thought of as impassible, with difficult-to-find paths that seemingly disappear midway through, harsh terrain, and music like that of a piano, encouraging you to return to the base of the mountain. Many have made the journey into the mountains looking for game or gold, only to never return. We don't know if they died, got lost deep in the caves, or perhaps found a better life out in the great beyond, but many of us presume they are no longer with us, unfortunately."

Violet, nervous, then asked, "Where are the mountains? I don't see them in the distance like I would expect to—are they far away? Are they too small to see? Are they snow-capped or green? I don't want to die, get lost, or go missing, but I do want to save the world and the power source needs to be shut down."

Ruth, pausing a moment to think, sighed and then stated, "There is a great spell of Alice's that blocks the mountains from view until you get closer to them. This is to help prevent prospective explorers from attempting to scale them. There are some small villages near the base of the mountains, and I've heard whispers of a small community about halfway to the summit of the tallest peak, but it's straight ice after that and no one dares venture further. Despite it originating from Alice, we all try to hold the secret to prevent any newcomers visiting the mountain…it isn't worth the risk and we should find another way to access the power source if possible. Perhaps a lake or stream in the Great Woods near the mountains would give us the answers we seek? Or perhaps a different way into the mountains exists, through a tunnel or below ground passage that might feed into the caves? The mountains are so dangerous that we have never dared look for alternate routes—the magic is too strong and the risk too great."

Violet, feeling determined, replied, "We should visit the library and read more about this. There has to be a path forward. But Alice still needs to be destroyed. We need to prepare ourselves because she will be expecting us." Violet returned home for the night, feeling like her life might be looking up for once.

Having decided to join Ruth and Violet on their journey to the mountain region, Allen asked Violet if he could spend an evening alone with her—just the two of them—before they set off. They had dinner in the quiet private room of the chophouse, eating chop suey: Allen's with beef and mushrooms, and Violet's with double mushrooms instead of meat. After expressing their fears of the unknown as well as their determinations for restoring the portal between worlds, Allen took a moment to breathe before saying, "I have grown to admire and cherish you deeply, and I wish to ask you a question that is of great importance to me." From a small box, he pulled out a ring—yellow gold, with a rectangular ruby complete with one small diamond on each side of it. Visibly tearing up slightly, he then continued by saying, "My dearest Violet, for some time now, I have had the great fortune to know you, to admire your grace, your kindness, and the beauty of your spirit. In you, I have found a true companion, someone who makes my days brighter and my heart fuller. There is no greater joy in my life than the thought of spending my future by your side. I come to you now with the most earnest of intentions, and with a heart filled with love and hope. I humbly ask for the honor of your hand in marriage, to walk through life together, side by side, sharing all that it may bring. Will you do me the great honor of becoming my wife?"

Having been hoping for this moment, she smiled and responded, "I would be honored to accept your proposal."

The next morning, Goosey decided to tag along as well, although Ruth expressed concerns about a goose crossing mountainous terrain, even if she felt Goosey could fend for herself. Violet, Allen, Ruth, and Goosey set their sights eastward, towards the mountains that, though not yet visible in the distance, seemed to beckon them closer. Each step took them further from their known world, the western portion of the magical realm fading away as they headed towards the unknown.

The land stretched out before them, laying barren and empty, interspersed with stretches of forested areas and fields adorned with colorful flowers. From time to time, they spotted a goblin or another being traversing the terrain in the distance. Whenever they encountered someone close enough, they exchanged friendly waves, but they were grateful that no one wanted to stop and talk. As they walked, the path transformed, with the gentle slopes becoming more pronounced. The fog remained in the distance, and they were unable to see the mountains through it yet.

As days passed, growing purple and black over and over again, the air grew thin and crisp, the horizon shifting and changing as fog began to cover their sight in all directions. Yet with each step further, the mist began to retreat, unveiling the beautiful mountain peaks that stood tall against the violet sky. They grew concerned, not knowing what destiny awaited. Violet remembered that many had ventured into the mountains and never returned, and she feared that those numbers might include them in the near future.

The mountains loomed closer with each passing hour, no longer just shapes in the distance, but real and right in front of them.

Upon reaching the foothills, they paused—the last remnants of fog dissipating. The entrance to the mountain awaited them, a gateway to a realm spoken of only in rumors. They approached from the south, a route rumored to be safer and offering the easiest access to the caves.

The journey wound upward and around, each turn revealing more of the majesty and great blue and white of the mountains, despite the dark purple tinge left by the ever-dark.

Allen was becoming visibly concerned, appearing less and less happy about helping Violet. She had been noticing that he hadn't smiled with his eyes in a while and was not as expressive. As they were about to leave their known world, she grew worried that Allen might leave her as well.

As they approached the entrance to the caves, which lead to the Mountain Kingdom, an apparition of Kazuki appeared. "Violet, you must know that there is no stepping back from this moment. Once your journey occurs, the time equilibrium will be forever equalized. There is no changing what will happen if you continue on your quest down this path. Please be prepared, and find Chuyi as she will help you while I cannot." He then faded into oblivion.

Looking to Ruth, who had long provided insights, Violet asked "Ruth, do you know what Kazuki meant by that? Who is Chuyi?" Sighing, Ruth said that she did not know what he meant by that, but she had her theories about the power source ahead of them and would prefer to not jinx anything for the time being. As for Chuyi, Ruth felt that she was most likely a friend of Kazuki's as she wasn't familiar with the name.

With Violet and Goosey ahead of Ruth and Allen, they entered the cave they believed led to the Modern Realm, not knowing what to expect. A moment of ripples occurred, and then they walked through a black field filled with streaks of lightning in slow motion for several minutes.

CHAPTER 6

Loud and bright despite the cavernous structure, they appeared to be in another time or perhaps another universe. Lights were everywhere, with no sign of gas lamps. The lights formed large words and signs. There were tall, multi-story buildings filled with words written on the sides. Some were readable in English, while others were written with scrawled characters that must have been in an alien language.

All around her, the air hummed with an unnatural sound. The lights from the foreign characters flickered and buzzed, as if the light itself was alive or powered by a great spell. Is this how the inhabitants attempted to counteract the ever-violet or black sky? Was all of this built after the portal closed? The lights mimicked daytime, although the sun had not been seen since the portal was shut. The buildings around her stretched higher than she thought possible. There were whooshes under her feet, which made her stumble as if an earthquake rippled below her.

Coming to her senses, she began to notice more sights and sounds around her. Above and in front of her, metal carriages moved by, faster than wild beasts but with no horses in sight. Honking and screeching, they rushed past faster than the speed of light. And the people—hoards of them—moved by in waves, faster and more crowded than any market or village event she had ever seen. One thing they all seemed to have in common was their uniform hair: sleek, straight, and white hair, a great contrast to the shades of black, brown, blonde, and occasional red from her hometown and the magic world. White hair wasn't unheard of, but was rarely seen and reserved for the elderly, yet there was only white uniformity here. How would they ever fit in when everything there was stranger, louder, brighter, and more bustling?

"Is this the true meaning of modern?" Violet thought to herself. Unsure what to do, Violet looked to Ruth for reassurance. Despite her usually calm demeanor, she appeared nervous and deep in thought. "Where are we? Are we on the planet or are we out there somewhere else in the universe? *When* are we? I don't understand these inventions. I am so confused." Violet said to her. As if in answer to her silent prayers, a newspaper floated down from above, possibly coming from the great bridge above her, where some of the metal carriages whooshed by, although some were in the sky and some were at ground level as well. Hesitantly, she reached down and grabbed the newspaper. More strange characters appeared, and full color—not just black. There was English too, although she didn't understand every word. Leaning closer to Ruth and turning the paper, they tried to make sense of this place. The headline stated *Aria Times*, and the upper right corner told them that the year was 2050, almost 200 years after their time. After a moment, her jaw dropped—her old neighbor, Andrew, with his zany neuroticisms was right; there was a land called Aria. She wondered how he knew of its existence. Unsure how any of what she was experiencing was possible, she broke into tears.

Ruth then admitted, "Violet, this is what I had feared. I had heard whispers of the time continuum and every place not existing in the same time. Kazuki may be right —I believe that our actions may have unintended consequences."

As they continued to look around, Violet noticed posters nailed to fixtures often, as far as her eyes could see. In English, and seemingly in the illegible characters as well, was the word "Wanted" with Alice's portrait on every poster nailed to every fixture she could see. "Hundreds, thousands even..." Violet whispered. "Why so many?" she asked aloud.

Wondering what specifically Alice was wanted for, they pulled down one of the posters and began to seek out someone who might have information. They set off in what they believed was the northeast direction, looking for someone kind enough to help as the hoards of people passed by, and metal beasts screeched by in every direction. As they crossed the next street and began to see openings in the caves, leading to a continuation of the city out in the ever-dark, a woman with a metal left arm, complete with ball joints and two wheels where her feet should be, said, "I've been expecting you."

Confused, worried, and wondering how that would be possible, Violet asked "And how is that? Who are you?"

The woman stated, "I am Chuyi, a longtime acquaintance of Kazuki's. We are two of the spiritual guides across the realms and connected in ways you would not understand. I was deeply saddened to hear of his passing, but grateful in a way since he led you all to me."

Ruth, grateful that they had found her as she thought highly of Kazuki, ran up and hugged Chuyi, despite not understanding her body's mixture of metal and skin. Realizing she should ask about that, Ruth asked, "Chuyi, why are you part machine like the beast-like carriages we have seen around the modern realm?"

Chuyi responded, "Ah, I sometimes forget about the pressing spells of magic that seal us in. I am a cyborg, kept alive by modern science and medicine, after a great carriage accident when I was younger. There are many of us scattered around, we are nearing 20% of Aria's population. I am truly grateful, as modern technology allows for some of us on the brink of death, such as myself, or others who are not, to receive care through technology instead of just old-fashioned medicine that you may be accustomed to. Instead of a drink of tea or some balm applied to a wound, we can be fixed with electronic technology that you may not be familiar with, such as wires, computers, machines, and metal."

Wanting her to get to the point, Violet nearly yelled, "And why is Alice wanted? We know all too well of her evils, but what has she done here?"

Chuyi sighed, responding, "Alice is Queen of the Witches, yes, but she struggles to understand that she has no authority here as we are an autonomous realm. Many centuries past, she began a massacre of anyone she believed would challenge her rule. Catching a glimpse of what would one day be our technological advancements, she cast a spell to keep the rest of the magical realm and the entire mortal realm in the past. Because of this, there is a great fog amidst a forcefield. None from our lands are able to leave. When we approach the Great Barrier, as it is called, we are physically unable to leave. When others journey here, they are able to enter, but unable to leave. This prevents the challenging of her rule. However, what she may not understand is that her closing of the portal means that the mortal realm is in the modern era now, unable to ever return, even if the portal re-opens. Yet, the closing of the portal had great consequences, as the magical realm gets its energy from the mortal realm. Now Aria is cast in deep purple, and we do not know if that will change unless her or her blood chooses to destroy the forces kept in the Walled City. There is a great source of power sealed with her blood, and only her death and the destruction—by her blood—can overrule this. Alice is wanted here, dead or alive, as they believe her death will allow us to leave our kingdom as we used to. She is not stupid enough to venture here though, for although she is the only person who we know can come and go, she knows we are a force to be reckoned with if she ever shows her face. Rumor has it that she sometimes visits the power source to ensure it is functioning, but she leaves before anyone is able to take her out."

They grew concerned for Violet, as she appeared to be frozen. She had just learned she would never see her hometown in the time period she grew up in; she hoped Chuyi was wrong and that there was a way to restore the portal without affecting the mortal realm's time. "Why are you traveling with a goose by the way?" Chuyi cheerily asked no one in particular, as if she didn't possess the feeling-reading tendencies spiritual guides were meant to.

Ruth sighed, wanting to exit the conversation, and replied, "It's complicated."

After the conversation with Chuyi, Violet, greatly distressed, fell and skinned her knee. She would've been content to just keep walking, but Allen was concerned and there was an infirmary up ahead, so they stopped in to get her knee looked at. After a mind-boggling long questionnaire and a back-and-forth discussion, the physician stated that Violet had major depressive disorder and complex post-traumatic stress disorder, whatever that meant, but the knee was just scraped so she could go home after it was sterilized. Violet tapped the stack of papers against her leg and waited to have her scrape cleaned so that she could go.

Staring up at the ceiling late at night, Violet looked over at what she now knew was called a nightstand. The clock stated 2:00 AM. Tears rolled down her eyes. "I do not know when it is," she thought to herself. Allen was asleep and seemed content, but she could not accept that her calm village lived 200 years in the past. She could not accept that things were so different and that the existence of a so-called "modern" world meant that she lived in the past, unaware of the future, or perhaps the present, so close by. She did not know what had caused all of this, but it was deeply upsetting to her. She could not sleep. She still had nightmares of her sisters, but they had been fading in the recent days. She feared for what would happen if she opened the portal to her home world. Would time still exist as she knew it? She knew she should go to bed, but-she often could not find the point of sleep as she was filled with so much sadness. She did not know if Allen really loved her, or if he just loved that she loved him. She did love him and wanted to become his wife, but she wasn't sure if he wanted that of her. "Enough thinking for the night," she thought to herself.

The following day, Ruth and Goosey began to prepare for battle as they did not fully know what to expect when confronting Alice, and they wanted to be prepared for any possibility. While Ruth was practicing her magic and Goosey was preparing in her own way, Violet went with Allen in search of a weapon shop. After walking up and down a few streets, they entered a store called "Discrete Weaponry," which was staffed by a male cyborg who introduced himself as Kengo. They browsed the selection with Kengo's help, and Allen purchased a sword as well as two daggers. Violet did not have much practice with her magic, so she bought two daggers and two throwing stars to protect herself as well. To be safe, they grabbed a dagger for Ruth as well. On the way out of the store, they ran into Chuyi again, and she must have been more of a mind-reader than they thought as she had a longsword strapped to her back.

"Today is the day that Alice will be defeated, is it not?" Chuyi asked, before offering to join the group in their efforts to save the world. The three of them walked back to where Ruth and Goosey were practicing and briefly tested out their weapons. Violet spent around an hour practicing her wind magic with Ruth's help as well. Then, despite feeling underprepared, they set off towards The Walled City, which contained the power source. Chuyi explained that they would need to take a form of transportation known as a train, which was essentially a very large carriage that could carry many people at fast speeds, along a known route. They discussed battle strategies while following Chuyi's lead across the city, until they arrived at the C Line Station.

When Violet and her companions approached the C Line Station, an underground transit station that operates the line heading to the Walled City, the conductor—who was used to opening and closing the transit doors while smoking opium, the easiest job in the territory—ventured out of the conductor's car to ask why they were at the station as the route only existed to appease the administration. After hearing that they were there to go to the Walled City, he squeaked "But why? Are you sure?" His hands fidgeted nervously, and his eyes widened with hesitation, before he quickly turned and retreated to his post at the front of the train. Chuyi tapped a small rectangle five times as they were boarding the train and explained that she was paying the fare for each of them. At the last and never-used stop, he once again tried to admonish them by saying "The train turns around here. I can take you back downtown free of charge." They ignored him and got off at the Walled City's train station.

The Walled City's train station was once a crucial piece of infrastructure that would allow passengers from the Walled City to travel throughout Aria. Now, it was not in use, although Aria's administration had required all routes to run as scheduled. This meant that day in and day out, every 15 minutes an empty train departed from Downtown Aria before concluding and reversing just about a half mile outside the Walled City's gates. If history unfolded differently, transit might have run into the Walled City's territory as well, but for now the last stop—rarely taken—resulted in a ten-minute walk to the gate. At Chuyi's direction, they began walking towards the Walled City.

CHAPTER 7

Slowly and hesitantly, they approached the Walled City. Known for being dark, ominous, and filled with nefarious acts, it was not a good place to be caught in the ever-dark. Off to the side of the path leading to the city was a small cemetery, and a small prickle on the right side of Violet's head led her to feel that they needed to investigate the cemetery. "I need to look at something for a quick moment," Violet said to the group. They followed her, and after passing by a large oak tree, they approached the first row of graves, but Violet's instincts were guiding her to the third row of the cemetery, near a small bench. Kneeling by a grave that seemed to call out to her, she peered down and read "Andrew Wilcox—Born October 16th, 1852, Died January 7th, 1910. 'I made it to Aria.'" Violet spoke softly, almost to herself. "This cannot be right."

Chuyi walked over and paused, looking at Violet.

"What's wrong? Do you know this person? This is an old cemetery, Violet. Rarely passed through."

Violet, still surprised, responded, "He was my neighbor. I always wrote him off as being crazy, but we had spoken before I shut the portal and he told me he was going to Aria. Maybe I should've believed him, but how is he here? How is he dead? Shouldn't he be alive and well just like myself? Or did he somehow cross after the portal shut, and time didn't know where to place him?"

Chuyi, despite being a guide to the realm, felt baffled. "I don't know, Violet, and I don't know if we ever will know. Alice is unstable and could have done many things to allow this to happen. All I can say is that he seemed grateful for making it to Aria."

This discovery served as a powerful reminder of not just human resilience and dreams, but also that others may know more than you do and that we should not always count people out, Violet thought to herself. She never believed Andrew's ramblings of Aria, thinking he was not quite right in the head, but maybe she shouldn't have doubted him to the level she did. She felt like this was a major turning point for her—tangible proof that she could do anything she set her mind to.

As they neared the Walled City, a foreboding, tall, black castle with three turrets loomed in the distance, casting a great shadow over the city. It was said to otherwise contain slums, and of course, it harbored the power source directly in the middle of the city. They approached the Walled City's gates, and they eerily swung open for them, hinges creaking. Alice's cackling could be heard from the exterior of the wall, truly show-casing her insanity.

Once they reached Alice, the air grew tense, as if it were charged with electricity. Alice stood tall, her eyes locked on Violet, and taunted, "Violet, Violet, Violet. You think you can best me? And who is this?" She walked over to Goosey. "A strange-feeling goose? You should give up now."

Violet began to sense something stirring inside her avian friend, as Alice had, but she couldn't quite put her finger on the sensation, despite the closeness she shared with her.

A great battle ensued when Ruth threw the first blow, protecting Goosey. After a clash with traditional weapons and magic, fire exploded from Goosey's mouth and vanquished Alice. Not knowing that Goosey possessed magic, Violet felt greatly surprised and began to wonder if that was what had caused the strange feeling.

After Alice's death, her body shriveled into a husk, slowly burning away until she turned to dust and eventually blew away, while the victors watched mesmerized. After the last speck of what was once the world's greatest terror had drifted off, something very unexpected happened. Goosey, Ruth's longtime companion and Violet's new confidant, began to shimmer and radiate with light unlike anything even the Modern Realm had seen before. A metamorphosis began to occur, with Goosey slowly shifting before Violet's eyes. Her feathers began to disappear, her wings replaced by arms, and her orange webbed feet turned to human ones. Soon after that, a young girl tumbled to the ground, where Goosey had been but minutes before.

Ruth, with fearful looking eyes, turned to Violet. Holding up her hands in a "stop" gesture, she exclaimed, "I can explain."

Betrayed and confused, Violet was admittedly very bewildered. "Ruth, why did your goose friend turn into a child? How could you have kept that from me? I have confided a lot in Goosey, not to mention that I blew her into a tree!"

Ruth shook her head, looking distraught. "It's a secret I hoped I wouldn't have to take to my grave, Violet. This is your younger half-sister, Scarlet. She is ten years old."

Violet shook her head, saying "No, I have two sisters, neither of which like me."

Ruth shook her head in response. "Violet, I understand if you don't want to speak to me after you hear what I have to say, but your younger sister is innocent. Your father, Bal, and I were having an affair when Alice killed him, along with your mother, hoping to protect herself from usurpment. It wasn't until after your father passed that I discovered I was with child, and to protect Scarlet after her birth, I turned her into a goose. No one else knew of her existence or my pregnancy, to be frank, so those who knew me thought I had adopted a small gosling and chose to raise her as a friend. I couldn't risk Alice's wrath myself and lived in fear of her discovering another Evans, so it was the only thing I could think to do other than hide her away. Even then, I feared Alice would recognize her own blood, and I wouldn't be able to get to my dear daughter in time or even know what had happened. At the time, a transformation was the only way I could hope to protect her." Kneeling down, Ruth pushed Scarlet's hair out of her face and rubbed her back. "Scarlet, can you hear me?"

Scarlet, having awoken as herself for the first time since her birth ten years past, sat up before asking, "Mother?"

As Alice and the power source were gone, the curse preventing the sun from rising was immediately broken. Day righted itself, and the sun appeared in the sky where it should have been the entire time.

CHAPTER 8

Feeling like her journey was reaching its end, Violet prepared to open the portal with Scarlet by her side. Pressing her hands into the blackness that once shimmered, the portal cracked open, exploding outward and pushing her back. Where the portal once lay, the land seemed to have fused together as one—allowing beings to pass back and forth in either direction without the need for a portal.

Violet looked forwards, backwards, and all around, and it was like her two lives had fused together. Hesitantly, she stood and brushed the dirt off herself, before approaching what was once the portal again. Cautiously, and as she expected, she was able to step through with Scarlet. Things were not as Violet had expected after the initial shock had worn off, though, and Circa was not as she had remembered. Part of where her beloved forest once lay, known for providing her comfort while reading, had transformed into a charming sanctuary for cats—

strays now reigned where towering trees once provided her comfort as she read for hours. This meadow, sprinkled with felines, now cradled her beloved Crater Lake, which glistened under the sun.

Looking past the remnants of her "peaceable spot" as she called it when she was younger, she noticed that hardly a trace whatsoever of her past remained. What was once her village was now devoid of life, appearing quite desolate and sad despite the felines who had made themselves at home. While there were some trees, much larger than she remembered, much of what she recognized was either gone, turned to rubble on the ground, or scattered in ruins throughout the grassy meadow that extended past what was once the forest. While she was greatly saddened by what she had discovered, she also felt mesmerized by the beauty of the expanse of nature, the rubble, and the ruins. In a sickening way, it was much more beautiful this way than with coldhearted people who caused her trouble. The rubble remains of buildings, towering ruins, tall grass, tall trees, and light rippling off the Crater Lake was beautiful in a way she could have never imagined previously.

Feeling a deep sense of otherworldliness and unease, Violet looked down to Scarlet for reassurance, but Scarlet just shrugged her shoulders. Feeling a concern for Isabella and Margaret's well-being despite their past, Violet told Scarlet to stay close while they walked towards what was once the village. Eventually, they did see a standing cottage in the distance, behind a small hill where the village apothecary once stood, and past a towering tree line that used to be much less striking.

As Violet approached, with Scarlet lingering slightly behind, the cottage door creaked open, revealing a flickering hologram of their sister Margaret stirring a cauldron inside. With a voice both ghostly and familiar, the hologram turned to Violet and said, "We've been waiting for you." The portal's reopening had returned Violet to a blend of what once was and an uncertain present. Were her sisters truly waiting, or was all lost to time?

As Violet stepped inside the cottage, she began to understand the truth of everything that had happened, while Scarlet remained outside, waiting. Over 200 years had passed between when she last walked through her village and now. Speculation from others on her journey must have been true, she thought to herself, as it appeared the time continuum had now set all connected realms to "modern" day, a place where she felt she may never fit in.

As Violet stood rooted to the spot, the ghostly hologram in front of her continued to flicker and speak. Margaret's voice, neither warm nor cold, cut through Violet's tumultuous thoughts. "Violet, we—well mostly myself—always believed that once the portal was shut, everything would change irreversibly. We missed you, despite pushing you away, something we should have never done. But Isabella... she always blamed you for the death of our parents."

The words hung in the air, suffocating in their weight. Violet's heart pounded, each beat reverberating with a mixture of pain and resentment. How could she have been unaware of the depth of her sisters' enmity?

Margaret's voice wove through Violet's consciousness. "I'm sorry we never made the circumstances clear. We suspected you might try to open the portal again, but believed we were better off with it shut. Alice... she couldn't torment us further then. She was always jealous of me, you know? Thought I would usurp her position." A hollow, mirthless laugh escaped the hologram. "As if I would ever desire such responsibility! To be candid, I wasn't thrilled about having a second sister either."

The confession stung with a sharp cruelty, lodging itself deep within Violet's wounded soul. She nodded numbly. The truth she had long sought blanketed her heart, causing her emotional pain to become psychosomatic pain felt strongly in the left side of her chest. Her hope for things to improve in the future shattered, and she began to understand that Margaret was far worse of a person than she had ever imagined.

"After she killed our parents, though, she mainly left us alone. We don't entirely know why, but we hadn't seen her since—may have been something to do with the portal's magic. We could go back and forth, and believe me, we did behind your back before you knew of its existence, but it seemed she wasn't able to return. Patricia and Bal's destruction must have been good enough for her...until you disappeared, and the portal shut. With our mode of entry sealed, she would never need worry about being usurped as you would never think to do such a thing—hah!"

"Anyway," Margaret continued with a hint of gravity, "we knew the time continuum would resolve itself when you reopened the portal yet hoped it would not—so we could continue to spite you. Though, truth be told, it meant we would never have to see you again and we were grateful for that. We burdened you with responsibility for actions that weren't yours. My apologies for that expression of grief and, frankly, ignorance. Though, I believe you understand that I could not care less about how it affected you."

Echoes of their separation raced through Violet's mind, relentless and unnerving. She had played peacemaker too long in a fractured family, a fragile and damaged girl surrounded by magical forces beyond her understanding. The realization weighed heavily on her as Margaret's words resonated.

"Isabella has long since passed. You didn't know we were witches at the time, and I imagine you do now, but I possessed what we considered the strongest magic in the family: a true witch. Even so, Isabella was envious, seeing more potential in you than herself! After all, when Alice murdered our parents targeting me, she blamed you—for what? For her grief, her belief in your latent powers?"

Each revelation made Violet feel as if she had been kicked in the shins, although she did feel a small boost in confidence after hearing that they had seen something in her she had never glimpsed in herself. She felt hurt that her "potential" had bred suspicion and hatred rather than connection, and that Isabella and Margaret felt the need to knock her down rather than lift her up.

This was a common theme throughout her entire life, and it was a large contribution to Violet's melancholy.

"The restoration of the continuum now means you won't ever see her again. The past is unreachable through dreams or reality," Margaret continued without hesitation. Her spectral presence suggested more permanence than the flesh-and-bone bodies Violet yearned for.

"I must apologize," Margaret added with detached sarcasm, "we kept this from you, hah! I remain, but don't mistake it for duty to reconnect—other than perhaps making you ponder your own actions." The hologram in its finality, with bits of static rippling its features, seemed more a ghost of grudges than a living memory. "You might find me near Isabella's grave, if curiosity drives you. But consider this hologram my final goodbye. See you never!"

With those words, Margaret's image faded, leaving Violet and Scarlet in stunned silence. Steam-like, the hologram disappeared, enveloping Violet in the chilling realization that time, indeed, heals nothing. Only memory and intention remained to influence what happened next. After the hologram's disappearance and Violet left through the doorway to return to Scarlet, the hut burst into flames. Violet and Scarlet stood by and watched, standing back to avoid breathing in the resulting smoke or ash, mesmerized at the magic that had led their eldest sister to spite Violet to this level, yet of course, they were greatly upset by it. Violet watched,

Scarlet at her side, until the house faded away and collapsed into itself, a great pile of ash.

Scarlet asked, looking up at Violet, "Why is our sister so horrible? You deserved so much better, Violet. You've been nothing but kind as long as I have known you," she said. The best answer she could provide at the moment was a shrug of her shoulders. In the consuming quiet, Violet understood her path was both clearer and more uncertain than ever; her journey—and their story—was far from over.

Bittersweet tears brimmed in Violet's eyes now, and spurred by the hologram's parting words, she felt an urgency to find Isabella's grave. She worried her quest had led her to a crossroad, where ghosts of the past revealed more than she had ever bargained for. Despite her diligent, seemingly hours-long search up and down hills, through meadows and around and between ruins and rubble with Scarlet by her side, all they encountered were cats weaving through the trees, leaves floating by, and rolling hills stretching into fields with no trace of humanity. The Crater Lake glistened, and while always beautiful, it now mocked her old life. The isolation of the place concealed any clue of where Margaret's cryptic hints might lead. Knowing Margaret, the grave was perhaps through another portal altogether, or across seas in lands uncharted, requiring a map she didn't possess, and she didn't have time to play games or attempt to venture further west. She still wasn't familiar with the geography of her homeland and did not want to venture into unknown danger with only a child.

Despite the hologram's claim at first sight, Isabella and Margaret had not truly been waiting. Feeling defeated and devastated, Violet accepted the situation and conceded. With Scarlet by her side, glancing up with reassurance, they returned to the remains of the portal. Violet's heart was heavy, but she was determined to end this journey for now and prepare for her wedding that would take place the following morning. She could always return with Allen, lending their combined strength to navigate her former home that had been transformed by time and regret.

Feeling greatly distressed, Violet passed through the space where the portal once was with her younger sister, ready to collapse into her bed. Violet knew her journey —and perhaps her answers—awaited further explorations, dwelling beyond the remnants of the portal she was leaving behind. Once on the other side, she helped Scarlet into the back basket of her tricycle and ensured she was strapped in before beginning to pedal home. She dropped her off with Ruth, then headed back to the cozy tenement house she shared with Allen. However, Allen was nowhere to be found. Knowing his mother lived not too far off, she considered that Allen may be staying there overnight to keep with the tradition of not seeing the bride the night before the wedding, or the morning of. "That is all it is, a simple tradition," Violet thought to herself, while the unease grew. Despite all of this, she drifted into a fitful sleep, attempting to get enough rest to make it through her hopefully memorable wedding day ahead.

CHAPTER 9

On her wedding day, Violet had a bad feeling deep inside herself, but thought it might just be from stress or anxiety. Allen must have just spent time with his mother, she thought to herself. She took some deep breaths, but even self-soothing didn't ease the tension brewing inside her. Regardless, she knew she had to get ready for the ceremony and was excited to spend her life with the man she loved. She donned her ivory dress and tied her bow in the back, feeling as though she shouldn't wear pure white due to her lack of purity. Confident in herself and her appearance, she told herself to stay positive as she started walking towards the local church. "It's just wedding day stress and nothing more," she thought to herself.

Walking in the door knowing she would have no one to escort her down the aisle, she was still glad to see the few guests that she invited seated around the church. Feeling sad that Kazuki and her friends and family—

except for Scarlet, who she chose not to blame for the circumstances of her existence—weren't able to attend, she still tried to keep a positive outlook. Grateful for Scarlet's presence, she felt glad to have someone in her corner. However, looking around, Allen was nowhere to be seen. She started to panic from deep inside herself, but kept her fear internal to prevent causing a scene at her wedding. Standing frozen at the front door hoping no one had noticed her yet, she fell to the ground in front of the door.

Several minutes later as she started to cry, Scarlet noticed her and knelt down beside her. "I'm sure he's just running late," she consoled her, "come sit with me in the meantime." Other guests noticed her sadness and expressed sympathy, feeling their own concern for Allen's whereabouts while choosing to internalize them out of respect for Violet. As the minutes turned into an hour, the entire church grew distressed. In an uproar, one guest shouted that they'd kill Allen for hurting Violet, although that was far from necessary.

Suddenly, a woman dressed in blue burst into the one-room building urgently asking for Violet, scroll in hand. Violet approached the woman who curtsied before handing her the scroll and made a quick exit. She unwrapped the twine and opened the parchment, which stated, "My dear Violet, I'm sorry but I can't marry you because I fear you aren't the woman I'm meant to be with. Take care of yourself, but this is the last you'll hear from me." Devastated and heartbroken, she fell to the floor in tears for the second time that day and was left to deal with abandonment yet again. Violet feared that despite her accomplishments, her life was over and she would end up alone in the end.

Not knowing what else to do with herself, Violet dropped Scarlet off with Ruth and then ventured to where Kazuki's accident occurred. She sat under the tree for several hours in an attempt at self-soothing, but began to feel an overwhelming sense of guilt. She hadn't asked him the important questions—where did he live? Where was he from? How did he know Chuyi? Did he have family? How did he become a guide? And why had he turned to opium? The weight of these unanswered questions made her feel selfish for never considering his personal life more deeply. She was determined to find his grave—if one existed—once her life had settled down.

CHAPTER 10
ALLEN

"I could not do it," Allen thought to himself as he paced back and forth in his mother's sitting room. Looking back through their relationship, he quite often felt that he had to support Violet on her quest to save the world, and deal with peril and the fear of death when he wanted to live a simple life as a worker at the canteen.

Thinking back to a moment he remembered vividly, while walking toward the unknown—what they would later come to know as Aria—he recalled hanging his head and sighing. He knew Violet was doing the "right thing," but he was not quite sure if it was the right thing for him. As they went to face off with Alice, he did not want to pick up a sword. He wanted to be baking bread or handing customers their change, yet because of the woman he loved, he was driven across the world and back. He loved her, but he thought to himself that if Violet were truly the woman he was to marry, he would not have those doubts in the back of his mind. Instead, they would have had the same path forward in mind. Violet also didn't want to have children, while he had always envisioned having a family of his own someday.

"I want to find order in this world, with or without Violet," Allen thought to himself. "However, that might mean helping Violet after she learns what has or has not happened on the other side of the portal. "Had I only not offered, or not been on shift that day..." he thought to himself. He would have never been involved with Violet or dragged through danger. Despite the frustration he felt toward Violet for her sense of determination, in the back of his mind, he knew there would never be another woman as wonderful as Violet.

CHAPTER 11

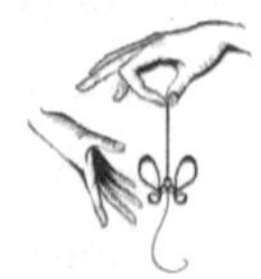

Violet knew she needed to be brave, despite feeling as if her world had fallen apart. She chose to stop by a local bar known for serving breakfast on weekend mornings. Sitting down on a barstool, she asked for the menu then perused it for a few minutes. Deciding on a light breakfast of cooked vegetables, two eggs, and a buttered baguette, she stared off into the distance while waiting for her food to arrive. After the server dropped off her plate and Violet was about to take her first bite, Ruth walked in and sat down next to her as Violet rolled her eyes.

"Violet, now listen to me. You must know I had my reasons to keep the knowledge of Scarlet's existence from you. I could not risk Alice learning she existed, and she has been known to have ways of extracting information from those she dislikes. I couldn't risk her hurting my daughter, but I am deeply sorry to have hurt you during the process. It was never my intention."

Sighing, Violet stated, "Ruth, I just want to eat my food. I don't know how you knew where to find me, but frankly, I don't care. I just want to eat my breakfast and then cry in peace. And then I guess I will move my belongings out of Allen's tenement house and back into the stable, unless I can find alternate accommodations on short notice. After that, I am considering putting more effort into finding Margaret, now that what was supposed to be my wedding day has passed, as I believe she should be informed of Scarlet's existence. Despite her not liking me, she should have the chance to know Scarlet should she so choose. Although, knowing Margaret, she will hate her as well on principle and honestly might traumatize Scarlet."

In response, Ruth stated, "Violet, I will support you in whatever capacity I can. If you would like to live in my house—even for the time being—you are welcome to stay with me. If nothing else, it would allow you more opportunities to bond with Scarlet. Consider it, please. If you need help finding Margaret, I can support you as best as I can on that front as well. I do agree she should meet Scarlet. Although, I admittedly have no leads, and I am not sure if anyone else would either."

Violet replied, "I will live with you if you will help me collect my belongings, and I will remain in your company until we have found Margaret and told her about Scarlet since I understand we have the same objective. After that, if I choose to no longer speak to you, I need your word that you will respect that and no longer be in my life."

Ruth pulled out a small pocketknife, cut her right palm, and held out her hand, saying, "Blood oaths are rare, but I agree to your terms. We will find Margaret and attempt to introduce her to Scarlet. After that, I will stay out of your life permanently if that is what you so choose. You have my word," and then she handed the knife to Violet who cut her palm in return and then shook Ruth's hand. Briefly, a black mark lit up on each of their palms, before fizzling out. Both of their cuts immediately healed and sealed over, leaving no trace other than the mental and magical ones.

They moved all of Violet's belongings into Ruth's third bedroom before Ruth stated, "I will be on my way now, Violet, and will be looking for leads into Margaret's whereabouts. Please don't wait up for me."

Violet chose to do the same—look for Margaret's whereabouts. She chose to do so through the pastime that had led her to this world to begin with: reading. She ventured to the library. She had been there many times before, and tonight, she was determined to find information on her eldest sister.

She dropped her bag onto a reading table and started her search, flipping through town registries that only appeared to be for those in the magical world, maps of the surrounding areas, and even old newspaper archives. Hours passed as she poured over every potential lead: articles about local disappearances, mentions of Witch Island and the Modern Realm, anything that might contain context to Margaret's whereabouts.

Nothing.

No trails, no clues, not even a fragment to follow. Margaret might as well have vanished into thin air when the time continuum righted itself.

Frustrated, Violet shoved the last newspaper back onto its shelf and sighed, glancing at the clock. It was nearing midnight. The castle library was next.

Venturing beyond the lever and the hidden curtain, she stepped into the castle's library. Was it hers now? Or perhaps it belonged to Scarlet? Violet frowned at the thought as she stepped into the room. She had always assumed Alice ruled everything, except for Aria, but now that Alice was gone, Violet realized she had never bothered to ask who truly held power over the kingdom. By law or inheritance, it could very well belong to her or Scarlet, unless there was another monarchy she was unaware of. Or... was it Margaret's, wherever she was?

"I need to ask Ruth," Violet thought to herself. Looking at the stack of books, she muttered to herself, "If there's anything on Margaret, it'll be here."

She began her search, pulling down leather-bound tomes and ancient scrolls. Names and titles blurred together as she scoured the pages, hoping for a clue about her whereabouts, or even a mention of potential hiding spots. The minutes bled into hours as the pile of discarded books grew higher, her frustration growing steadily.

Nothing. Not a single thread to follow.

Violet slammed shut a volume on "the lineage of enchanted blood" and leaned back against the desk she'd been using to research. The castle library had been her last hope, and it had failed her like everything and everyone else in her life. She decided to go back to her temporary home for the time being. She could always come up with another method of fruitless searching the following day.

Gathering her things, Violet made her way back through the secret passage and into the public library's comforting, familiar quiet. As she emerged into the night, she became very cold and hurried back to Ruth's. She could do little else now but wait until morning.

CHAPTER 12
RUTH

"Darn," Ruth thought to herself. Although she still understood the actions leading up to Scarlet's conception were wrongful to the Evans family, for all of Scarlet's life she had tried to protect her from harm. She had only done what she thought was best for Scarlet and what she felt would cause her the least harm. Perhaps she should have been open with Violet sooner, but she did not want to risk Alice learning of her existence and have the two of them be killed. As she walked to a nearby coven's dwelling—one that tried to stay under the radar and out of reach if one didn't know where to look—Ruth muttered to herself, "No, I did what was best, even if Violet does not see it that way right now." She intended to find Margaret, even if only for Scarlet's sake, as Margaret deserved to know of her sister's existence despite her cruelty to Violet.

Ruth decided to venture to the west, into the eerie

swampland not too far from her lake. The air grew thick with humidity, and the buzzing of insects accompanied her every step. The moss-covered trees twisted into unnatural shapes, their limbs filled with gnarled knots and dead leaves.

She began by speaking with a few white witches she encountered at the edge of the swamp. She knew that these witches had intentionally chosen to remain unaffiliated with Alice, aligning themselves with neither the island she once led nor her ideals. Despite Ruth's inquiries, they offered little help. They confessed that they seldom visited the mortal realm, having long abandoned those fleeting ties. They viewed the shutting of the portal as little more than an inconvenience, expressing concern only over the ever-dark that made it more difficult to participate in the activities they enjoyed each day. None of them could even recall hearing anything about Alice having family, let alone someone like Margaret. Their disinterest felt like a dead end.

Determined to not give up, Ruth made her way to Witch Island, a place she had hoped to not return to after Alice blew her and Violet off the last time she was there. She arrived at the modest home of Rowena, a former friend of Alice's. She had made a bit of a reputation for herself as a solitary witch who deliberately turned her back on covens long ago. The woman, though not hostile, remained guarded, her weathered features betraying decades of secrets she kept to herself. Momentarily, Ruth wondered why a witch such as Rowena would not return her features to those from her youth, but as she hadn't either, so she chose not to dwell on it. After pausing for a moment to ponder, Ruth beseeched her for answers, hoping to find some clue about Margaret's whereabouts. While this acquaintance admitted to having once known and even liked Alice, she too was unaware of Margaret's existence. The idea that Alice had family she despised came as both a surprise and a curiosity to Rowena, which greatly surprised Ruth.

The pattern was becoming maddeningly clear to Ruth—none of them knew anything. None of them cared to. They were disconnected from the mortal realm's struggles, their focus remaining rooted in survival after Alice's authoritarian leadership. Still, Ruth could not shake the sinking feeling that something was being hidden or left unsaid. She knew that other witches were aware Alice had a family, as Alice greatly feared being usurped. This was what led her to hide Scarlet as a simple goose many years ago, so she couldn't put her finger on why her fellow witches wouldn't talk.

In a moment of resolve, Ruth decided to check Alice's office within her black castle—the place where they had confronted her once before Alice kicked them off the island. The journey there felt heavy with foreboding, each step weighed down by the unease that could be felt deep in her bones.

When Ruth reached the office, her apprehension was confirmed. The space was unrecognizable. What was once a chaotic collection of Alice's notes, sigils, and tools of magic had been scrubbed clean. The walls were bare; shelves that once overflowed with tomes and artifacts now stood eerily empty. Even the faint traces of incense and magical residue had been erased. The room felt cold and sterile, as if someone had gone to great lengths to ensure nothing remained.

Ruth lingered, tracing her fingers along the barren surfaces, trying to find something—anything—that might have been left behind. But there was nothing. No stray parchment, no hidden marking. Whoever cleared this space didn't just remove its contents—they erased its presence, its soul. Ruth couldn't shake the unsettling questions that lingered in her mind: Who would go to such lengths to bury Alice's past? And why?

As a final attempt, Ruth decided to check Alice's former clothing shop. This visit felt more like a box to be checked, as the thought of finding anything there seemed unlikely from the outset. Sure enough, the shop was equally devoid of clues. The windows were still boarded, as Violet told her they had been. The mannequins stood lifeless, draped in dust-covered fabric, and the shelves were sparse. This emptiness, unlike the office, bore no mystery. It was to be expected, a hollow shell of the illusion Alice pulled over on Violet.

Ruth stood in the doorway of the shop, frustration and exhaustion weighing her down. Every lead had dissolved into nothingness, and all that remained were questions without answers. The sense of conspiracy surrounded her like the sanitation of Alice's barren office —a reminder that someone, or something, was working tirelessly to keep the truth out of reach.

CHAPTER 13
ALLEN

Allen had a conversation with Ruth, and after piecing things together, he realized Violet still felt furious with both of them. Frustrated and determined to uncover the truth about Margaret, he started reaching out to people he knew as well. At the canteen, he began casually chatting with the staff, probing for information. He also sought out other contacts: former classmates, his parents' friends, his mother, and anyone else who might have insight into the mysteries of the mortal world.

One day, during a shift at the canteen, a gruff-looking man took a seat near Allen. The man leaned in and said, almost conspiratorially, "I hear you've been asking questions about the mortal world. What do you want to know?"

Caught off guard but intrigued, Allen responded, "Have you been there since the portal reopened?"

The man shook his head. "No, haven't been. But I've heard things. What are you trying to find out?"

Allen hesitated but pressed on. "If someone were trying to hide out there, where do you think they'd go?" This line of questioning stemmed from what Ruth had admitted to him earlier: that they were still unable to locate Margaret. Desperate for clues, Allen explored every lead he could think of.

The man thought for a moment before replying, "About three days' journey west of the portal, there's an old abandoned lighthouse. It's known for being... well, foreboding, let's just say. Not many people go near it. From what I've heard and seen over the years, it's the kind of place someone might use if they didn't want to be found. I'd start there—or nearby."

The tip left Allen with a sense of both dread and determination. If Margaret was indeed hiding in the mortal world, this might be the breakthrough he had been looking for.

Allen approached Ruth's modest home, his steps heavy with weariness. Though a part of him was relieved that Violet wasn't there to meet him, another part simmered with frustration. He raised his hand to knock, but before his knuckles met the wood, the door creaked open on its own. As he entered, he was greeted by the sight of Scarlet sitting near the hearth. She held herself with an unsettling stillness, her posture almost too perfect, her movements deliberate, as though she were not yet accustomed to the body she now inhabited—a body she should have possessed all her life.

Scarlet glanced up at him briefly, her lips curving into a polite, if hesitant, smile. There was a certain tension in her demeanor, a quiet discomfort that Allen couldn't help but notice. He chose not to remark on it, instead lowering himself into a chair and waiting in the uneasy silence of the room until Ruth emerged from the kitchen.

CHAPTER 14

The sound of hurried footsteps broke the quiet, and the door swung open to reveal Violet. She strode in, her skirts rustling with each step, her face a picture of frustration. Tossing her bag onto the nearest surface, she let out a heavy sigh, her weariness plain to see.

"The library yielded nothing," she said sharply, addressing no one in particular. "Not a single lead, not even the faintest hint of where she might be. It feels as though we're chasing ghosts."

Allen exchanged a glance with Ruth before clearing his throat, his voice steady yet laced with urgency. "Actually," he began, his words carefully chosen, "we may have a lead."

Violet turned to him sharply, her frustration momentarily giving way to curiosity. "What do you mean? And why are you here?"

Ruth stepped forward, her voice calm yet firm. "Allen

has chosen to help search for Margaret. He has been speaking with various folk—acquaintances, coworkers, his mother, and even some old friends of the family. One man spoke of a possible lead... an abandoned lighthouse, three days' journey west of what remains of the portal. It has a reputation for being desolate, foreboding, and largely avoided by most. If Margaret is in the mortal world and wishes to remain hidden, it seems a likely place."

Violet's eyes narrowed as she absorbed the information, her weariness replaced by a spark of determination. "Three days' west of the portal's remains?" she repeated. "Then we had best leave now."

Ruth nodded, already gathering a few essentials for the journey. "It will not be an easy trek, but I have a good feeling about this. We'll depart as soon as we've made our preparations."

Allen shifted his gaze to Scarlet, who had remained silent throughout. Finally, she spoke, looking at Violet while attempting to keep her voice soft but steady. "I am nervous about meeting my eldest sister, especially because I can tell the thought of her is like a heavy weight dragging Violet down, but I know I need to go, so I will come as well."

The air in the room grew charged with purpose despite the worry clouding their thoughts as the four of them prepared for their journey. They each carried their own hopes and fears for what lay ahead, but Violet felt conflicted since she both hoped to make amends and never wanted to see Margaret again. The search for

Margaret Evans was no longer a futile effort—it was becoming a mission, with the faintest promise of answers waiting on the horizon.

They set out on their adventure, not knowing if their leads could be trusted, yet hoping they would find Isabella's grave and Margaret. They crossed through the boundary where the portal used to lay, arriving in the mortal realm. They paused briefly as Scarlet wanted to pet the cats that lived near the Crater Lake this time, and she asked her mother if they could bring one home with them. Ruth conceded, "Yes, but only one for now," although Violet felt she should adopt a feline companion as well.

They continued on their journey, passing the remnants of what was once the cottage containing Margaret's hologram; they followed the path Violet and Scarlet took on the first attempt at finding Isabella's grave. As they ventured further west, they first encountered a vast, eerie desert. Unlike any natural landscape, this desert seemed man-made, as if to spite Violet, an eerie expanse of black sand stretching to the horizon, under a sunless, grey sky.

As they trudged through the dense sand dunes, the ground beneath them shimmered with a metallic sheen, puzzling and unsettling in its unnatural beauty. Their footprints left dark impressions that shifting sands quickly swallowed, each step masking their path. The air was still, save for the occasional trickling of sand moving down the dunes. Every so often, they passed a scorpion. These creatures, unlike those found in the natural world, bore glistening, metallic claws and stingers, seemingly engineered for swift, silent aggression. While far different in personality, they were reminiscent of the cyborgs found in Aria. "Did technological advancements happen in my home world as well?" Violet thought to herself as the group continued to move cautiously. Every step was calculated and deliberate; they had to be ever mindful of the danger lurking beneath the surface.

After two days under the deep silence of the desert, they reached the outskirts of an oasis. The black sand stretched here as well, but occasional trees, and some grass patches greeted them as well. Despite a few standing buildings, most of the landscape consisted of rubble. Violet thought to herself "Is this what the modern world is truly like? Nothing but abandoned buildings and rubble?" They stopped briefly near a pool of water to relax, wash up, and drink before spending another day walking west.

Despite surroundings devoid of signs of life, they continued on until they reached the outskirts of a great apple orchard. However, the orchard as a whole felt far from welcoming. Despite their beauty, the trees were much taller and the wood much darker than what would be expected. The apples that hung from the branches were unlike any they had seen before, gleaming with a deep purple hue. They were alluring, and the color was very reminiscent of the ever-dark. Violet grew visibly uncomfortable, but she did not externalize what she thought about to her companions. "Why does everything bad turn purple?" she wondered bitterly. It felt as though the universe itself was a great marionette theater playing out an elaborate drama with her at its center and those who should love her pulling the strings. The ever-dark skies, the purple apples, and the creeping sense of unease and desolation in what was once her home world made her feel as if she was a magnet for calamity. Allen noticed Violet's distress and attempted to comfort her by laying a hand on her arm. Feeling conflicted, Violet replied, "Give me some time, okay?"

It was becoming palpable that Scarlet's proverbial feathers were ruffled as well, reminiscent of her time as a goose, and she worriedly stated, "I fear that the apples are poisoned, we need to move out of here quickly." Entering the purple orchard, Violet, Scarlet, Ruth, and Allen chose to make haste since they instinctively knew something was deeply wrong with their surroundings, even if their thoughts differed on what, specifically, was wrong.

In the heart of this harrowing orchard, a gentle encounter provided them with a glimmer of hope. A little girl, appearing to be around eight years old, her eyes wide and curious, peeked out from the shadows. As she stepped into view, her small frame made the group feel they could trust her. The girl regarded them with a surprising mix of innocence and intelligence, wise beyond her years. "Can I help you?" she asked, her voice soft yet piercing, cutting through the night.

Grateful for any assistance, they inquired about an old lighthouse to the west of the orchard. A sad look appeared on her face, and the girl nodded. She spoke of how the once proud structure that helped fishermen come to shore had crumbled to rubble long before she existed. Yet, she assured them that it was another day's journey at best. Understanding the value of such information, Scarlet offered her some chocolate as a bribe. She accepted the gift with a nod, promising her silence and disappearing between the trees just as the first rays of dawn began to rise—one of the first true sunrises they experienced after the ever-dark.

Violet, Scarlet, Ruth, and Allen pressed on, feeling better about their journey after the girl's guidance and the anticipation of finding the lighthouse, despite the deep sense of unease growing inside all of them. They managed to leave the area safely and felt a renewed sense of motivation. Each step west brought them closer to finding Margaret but deeper into the unknown. Violet became introspective, wishing she had known more about the mortal world as she felt things had changed significantly since she left, but the knowledge of the mortal world was not widespread in the village she came from. She assumed there must have been other civilizations—everything couldn't center around her, right?

Another day passed, and while the lighthouse slowly appeared in the distance, Violet began to apologize to the group as she had led them into this mess. Ruth responded, "This is our journey too, Violet. I want Scarlet to be able to meet Margaret, although I don't have much faith in your sister."

As they walked the path toward the lighthouse, Violet's gaze turned toward the horizon, a quiet determination in her eyes. She paused and felt gratitude for the return of the sun and turned to the others to see if they felt the same, yet they all appeared to be focused on the path ahead of them.

Violet's voice quivered while she said, "Before we confront Margaret, I want to find Isabella's grave. I need to see her and try to understand."

Scarlet shifted nervously beside her, tightly squeezing her mother's hand. "I've never seen a grave before. It feels scary, but I want to know where she is even if it makes me sad and I know she wasn't a good person."

Ruth removed her hand from the tight grasp and then gave Scarlet's hand a gentle squeeze. "It's okay to feel nervous, but you're braver than you know—after all, you lived as a goose."

They all continued down the path until they spotted a clearing under a stone pine. The grave was visible, tucked between small patches of bushy grass, its weathered headstone protected by the tree's protective branches. Allen looked to Ruth, wishing that Isabella was alive for Violet's sake, and said "we'll hang back, give you two some privacy. Ruth and I will be close by if you need us."

Violet and Scarlet stopped a few steps away, hesitating as Ruth and Allen settled on the ground beneath the pine.

"Take your time," Ruth said gently.

Violet glanced at Scarlet. "Are you ready?" she asked.

Scarlet nodded. "I think so," she said.

Violet and Scarlet approached the grave slowly, kneeling before it. Violet reached out, brushing her fingers over the dirt-covered stone to reveal Isabella's name. "Isabella Evans, builder of the desert," it said. "She's here," Violet said, her voice filled with sadness. "But why would she have built a black desert filled with scorpions?" She asked aloud, as it didn't make sense. Even if Isabella never liked her and built a land filled with creatures almost wretched as she was, Violet still wouldn't wish death on her own sister.

Scarlet looked down at the grave. "Do you think she's watching over us?" she said quietly.

Violet pondered and then shook her head. "I don't know, I don't think so. But I think she'd want us to remember her, even if she didn't like me."

Scarlet started to cry and rubbed her hand along Isabella's engraved name. "I'm glad I know where she is," she whispered. "Even if she wasn't a good person, she's still my sister."

Violet smiled and placed a hand on Scarlet's shoulder. "You're a good sister, Scarlet. Better than she and Margaret ever were to me."

They lingered by the grave, Violet giving her younger sister time to process until Scarlet stood, brushing off her knees. "I'm ready now," she said, looking at Violet. "Let's go find Margaret."

Violet stood as well, glancing back at the grave one last time and blinking back tears before turning toward the lighthouse. "Let's go," she said, her voice steady. Violet and Scarlet walked hand in hand to where Ruth and Allen were sitting, and the two of them stood up. Allen walked over and hugged Violet, while Scarlet ran into Ruth's arms. Violet addressed the group, "Isabella was the one who built the desert, I wonder if it was intended to keep me away if the portal was ever restored." Allen replied that while we could never know her true intentions, he was very sorry she had to think about things like that.

After a moment of silence, they turned their attention to the lighthouse, stark against the gray sky. They all approached, but Scarlet was afraid and hung back a step.

Violet and Ruth knocked on the front door of the lighthouse where they believed Margaret was staying, gently calling out "Margaret?" with Allen silently comforting Scarlet who was hiding behind them.

They heard shuffling on the other side of the door before Margaret, now an old crone who hadn't masked her age with magic, opened the door, broomstick in hand, and angrily said, "Why are you here? I am not responsible for you not having understood the location of Isabella's grave. She would not want you to visit anyway, so best be on if you are seeking directions."

Violet stepped forward. "No, Margaret, we already found the grave. I would like to offer a fresh start and try to reconnect with you, not just for myself, but for our little sister Scarlet."

Margaret replied, "There are no sisters of mine now that Isabella has perished, and she became no sister to me as well about 100 years after you left us. I will never forgive her for cursing my land with black sand after my reign started." Violet was truly flabbergasted to hear that her sisters weren't much different from Alice, as if the apple truly didn't fall far from the tree.

Scarlet stepped forward now, feeling brave despite her young age and determined to be nothing like her oldest sister. She spoke up for herself, "I am your younger half-sister. Ruth, the lady with Violet and I, is my mother. My father was Bal, your father as well. I am your blood, Margaret. Make of that what you will."

Margaret, forever stubborn, shouted, "I don't care and would rather perish than ever interact with relatives again." She then took her broomstick, and with her eyes wide, shoved it straight through her heart. What a graphic site, but it gave Violet closure as she now knew she wasn't the problem. However, Scarlet felt as if this memory would stick with her.

As if Margaret was what was holding the abandoned lighthouse over the harbor together, the lighthouse began to crumble, disintegrating before their very eyes, as rocks and rubble began to fall off the cliff behind it and into the sea.

After giving her a few moments to process what she just saw, Allen got down on one knee in front of Violet and apologized profusely, saying, "I'm so sorry for putting myself above your kindness and mission to save the world, Violet. Before I had met you, my only aspiration was to work at the canteen and live a quiet life. I hope you can understand why it was difficult for me to put my life on the line, and I understand if you will never forgive me for standing you up on our wedding day. It's not that I didn't want to be with you, and I'm sorry it took me longer than it should have to realize you are the reason for my existence. You are the air that I breathe, the blood in my veins, the sun, the moon, and all of the stars in my no longer violet sky. You are everything I could ever ask for or dream of. I promise to stick by your side, no matter what. Violet, will you be my wife?"

Violet, trusting her own judgment, said, "Not now, Allen, but maybe someday."

"I MISS LOOKING
AT BANANAS"

I miss being at the grocery store
Standing in the aisle
Looking at bananas
Deciding if I want
Green, yellow, or brown
Organic or regular
Small or large
And how many
I didn't know the importance of freedom
Until it was gone

- El Hoffman

ACKNOWLEDGMENTS

I would like to thank Heather Hoffman-Seifert, Melissa Mozingo, and Kate Ashford for supporting me as initial readers. I would also like to thank Sam Bolano for his work as my illustrator. Additionally, I would like to thank my former English professor Kevin Jett for acting as my proofreader. Kevin, your support has always been invaluable, thank you for your continued faith in me.

I would like to thank my physical copy Kickstarter backers as well: Christy S., Eric Seifert, Mike Tingle, Chris & Melissa Mozingo, the Sandlins, Eric Edelstein, Larisa I., Anthony Paul Burgos, Judy Lane, Heather Hoffman-Seifert, Jordan Stiles, Brian M. Fraioli, Adam Stahl, and Stacey Lane.

Last but not least, thank you to my readers for allowing my vision to take root in your minds. I hope you enjoyed *The Ever-Dark* and its included poems. If you did, please consider leaving a review on Amazon and/or Goodreads.

ABOUT THE AUTHOR

El Hoffman (born February 8, 2000) is an author, poet, and data expert. A lifelong writer, she debuted with the literary fantasy novella *The Ever-Dark*. The novelette *The Scarlet-Dawn* serves as its direct sequel. El is also the author of the contemporary romance novelette *No Other Reason* and three poetry collections: *The Mirror, The Mask, and All I Ask*; *The Moon, The Tide, and All I Tried*; and *The Volcano, The Flame, and All I Became*. Her work has also been featured in multiple anthologies.

Outside of fiction, El has built a career implementing HubSpot for businesses and earned her Master of Science in Data Analytics from Eastern University in 2024.

In her free time, she enjoys reading ebooks, playing video games, taking long walks, and hula hooping.

instagram.com/elhoffmanauthor

amazon.com/author/elhoffman

linkedin.com/in/elofagoodtime

tiktok.com/@elhoffmanauthor

threads.com/@elhoffmanauthor

youtube.com/@elhoffmanauthor

www.ingramcontent.com/pod-product-compliance
Lightning Source LLC
Chambersburg PA
CBHW021433110726
47901CB00008B/2408